ENDORSEMENTS FOR BLOODSTONE

"With her new novel, BLOODSTONE, Stephanie Oyinki has accomplished a rare feat. She has combined courage, commitment and an abundance of talent to produce a book that will garner a following. At a relatively young age, it takes a certain amount of courage to embark on a creative venture and in particular decide on a novel of such considerable complexity and nuance. It requires a commitment typically found in older artists to see such endeavor to its fruition. Even more importantly, it takes a special talent and creative instinct to execute this robust vision. For showing a combination of all these qualities, Stephanie Oyinki deserves our admiration and applause,"

DEJI HAASTRUP
Author, A Rich Enabling Silence
General Manager, PGPA, Chevron Nigeria Ltd.

"Taut pacing... A Tension-soaked book that builds with each page ...A masterpiece edge-of-seat thriller from a girl who is in her teen! Steph is a masterful story teller with a vivid imagination that will make the likes of John Grisham, James Patterson, Sandra Brown, David Baldacci and other thriller and suspense authors scratch their heads!!! Stephanie's BLOODSTONE defines the word "Brilliant,"

LARA OWOEYE-WISE
Author, LOL ... Lessons of Life with Lara
Deputy Chief News Producer, African Independent Television

"Stephanie Oyinki is a rare talent nurtured in the fiery crucible of modern day Nigeria. Her first novel, Bloodstone, demonstrates Stephanie's remarkable ability to create compelling characters embroiled in a complex and riveting storyline. Join her on a fascinating journey of intrigue and mystery, I promise you will not regret it."

CHIEF ATIM ENEIDA GEORGE (Yeye Araba of Ile Ife)
Senior U.S. Foreign Service Officer, retired

"Stephanie Oyinki's use of language, imagery and dialogic is apt and suggestive of someone with a fertile imagination. She explores the nuances of teenage life captivatingly with its attendant rivalry, petty jealousy, mischief, emotion, friendships, parties and junk food. Stephanie Oyinki parallels Stephen King in her portrayal of horror; she is thus one emerging writer who holds a lot of promise. Her debut effort **Bloodstone** *is worth reading.*

FUNKE TREASURE DURODOLA
Author, Memories of Grandma
General Manager, Radio One 301.5 FM, (FRCN)

"Stephanie Oyinki's novel is bone chilling, heart stopping, and hair-raising. **Bloodstone** is a sensational piece tinted with romance, full of action, terror and suspense, filled with labyrinths of plots and a host of deadly characters. What is the Bloodstone? Does it wield a magical power? Is something sinister about the gem? What is the purpose of the five-metre-long golden casket and the murderous trolls? You need to read this novel, page by page, to put the puzzles together, and then you will understand why Thalia Throne, the cheeky lead character has to be slaughtered in a ritual to put her to an everlasting sleep. The ending is both pleasant and terrifying.

LANRE OGUNDIMU
Author, Tale of the Cow Tail & Other Stories
From the African Diaspora

"The author, Stephanie Oyinki has a personality that is admirable so much, that with her sense of purpose and courage she has carved out a niche of her own. During the launching of my Book, she played the role of introducing me to the audience and her captivating presentation revealed the great potentials that she possessed. Personally, there is no doubt that the sky is only the beginning for her and evidently, she will affect humanity positively. This piece of work "Bloodstone" by Stephanie offers great lessons and discoveries about teenage life. I am amazed at the wisdom behind it,"

ADA OKAFOR
Author, Driven By Passion

"I ran into Stephanie in 2011 during the first class of my book club, GAS. Though she was the youngest in the club, her captivating imagination filled with intelligent characters in her first write up showed a lot of promise as an author. Believable characters and compelling plots, which she definitely has, are crucial, but there is something particularly fulfilling about a teenager writing a story that actually sees the world through the eyes of teenagers. She was able to capture the trauma and joy of being a kid like no other young Nigerian author has ever done. Perhaps, that is the reasons why I believe she will endure. I am very glad to see that her first book, **Bloodstone** is finally here and certainly, it will engage and entertain anyone who reads it,"

EBI AKPETI
Author, God Has A Sense Of Humour

"This is an incredible masterpiece; the lines keep flowing until the last word. Stephanie, I await your next publication anxiously.... I also will love to have you review your book with us at the WIMBIZ book Club. Stephanie congratulations.

KASHIM SHA" AWANNATU
WIMBIZ, Book Club

Bloodstone

The Amazon Series

Stephanie Oyinki

BLOODSTONE
THE AMAZON SERIES

Author Credit: Stephanie Oyinki

iUniverse books may be ordered through booksellers or by contacting:

iUniverse
1663 Liberty Drive
Bloomington, IN 47403
www.iuniverse.com
844-349-9409

Because of the dynamic nature of the Internet, any web addresses or links contained in this book may have changed since publication and may no longer be valid. The views expressed in this work are solely those of the author and do not necessarily reflect the views of the publisher, and the publisher hereby disclaims any responsibility for them.

Any people depicted in stock imagery provided by Getty Images are models, and such images are being used for illustrative purposes only. Certain stock imagery © Getty Images.

ISBN: 978-1-4917-9177-6 (sc)
ISBN: 978-1-4917-9176-9 (e)

Library of Congress Control Number: 2016904200

Print information available on the last page.

iUniverse rev. date: 07/26/2021

CONTENTS

ACKNOWLEDGMENT

GOD, though I thought I had no talent, you have proved me wrong again.

I want to appreciate the following people for their help and support in the production of the Bloodstone.

I would like to thank my dad, for pushing me to do what I never dreamt of doing in a lifetime and for making my dream come true; and for my mum, though she discouraged me from many silly dreams, she saw great potential in me in the area of writing.

Thanks, goes to Ebi Akpeti for making me realize that there is more to writing a book than meets the eyes through the GAS writers' launch. May appreciation to Ada Okafor for giving me all the support needed and allowed me for a day to feel what it meant like to get your book out there.

If I forget this group of people, my book will never be complete. The class of Z 2014 / 2015 set and every Queen's College girl that ever supported me.

Special thanks to the editorial team, Lanre Ogundimu, Adeniji Olayiwola and Nnene Ezeah for their dedication and diligence.

Prologue

In the dense darkness that filled the room, Thomas clan groped blindly in the poorly lighted hallway towards the elevator door, slowly and hesitantly. His black leatherjacket on black jeans aided him to blend seamlessly in the background, with only his eyes glittering like that of an owl in the dark of the night. For one thing, Thomas hated surprises in his line of work, especially when it comes to someone keeping him in the dark for no obvious reason.

The sky was moonless, casting a weird gloomy shadow in the atmosphere, almost the opposite of the feeling excitement when the full moon is out. There was a creepy felling in the air not quite right to Thomas and He hated such a feeling, because from experience, something bad always happens whenever he feels this way.

The elevator door was old, showing obvious signs of abandonment from the last residents. As he pushed the open button to the elevator door, it made a cranking sound that could only belong in a cheap horror flick, as if warning you of an eminent danger.

That was how Thomas was feeling as he entered the shaft. This whole scene was just another flick of a grandiose horror set that seemed to get worse with every passing moment. He could not imagine exactly what he had gotten himself.

He wanted to make quick money but rather he got himself into big trouble. From the onset, he knew that the man he was now working for is a sham, but money spoke and boy, did it speak loud.

Nobody involved in the black market racket could claim not to have heard of the name of Thomas Clan and his legendary criminal reputation he has built in the underworld. If you ever had any loose ends during a racket, you know whom to contact. He is a fixer.

Thomas never left his work half done, but this time something had gone wrong and he felt as if he is digging his own grave from the very first day he started the contract. He tried so hard to get information about his client, but he could not come up with even a name, no fingerprint, no police record, no picture and nothing whatsoever.

It started with just a call, a deal, money transfer and a promise for more money after completing the job. It was like disappearing act and he did not like it one bit.

Thomas did not care about who you were or what you did as long as you delivered money. Though what his "faceless" boss had asked for had strange, enough pricked his sub-conscious, leaving him to be the one to judge. He cleared the sweat that has started dripping profusely down his face, like someone who is about to meet his creator as the elevator labored sluggishly down to the last floor.

Today was to be the first day since Thomas started dealing with this mysterious client of his that they will be meeting face to face. He had never been the type of person that gets scared easily, but on this particular occasion, there were eminently traces of fear oozing out of every vein in his body.

He was sweating profusely and fidgeting, though he trained in the military to be in control of himself when in an enemy territory and as a soldier in Afghanistan.

Fear is like a weapon, it could be dangerous if it is in the hands of the enemy. Thomas and other soldiers would have taught of locking in their fear but it had been an almost impossible task. Today Thomas appeared to have forgotten all about his training and he had lost control of his emotions without even realizing it.

Finally, the lift jerked to a halt and its rickety metal door cricked as if the gate of hell is forced opened to an unrepentant sinner. As Thomas stepped out, the temperature dropped at an unbelievable rate and blood rushed up my spine to my brain. His head suddenly felt bigger and heavier as if he had seen a ghost. In panic, he brought out his gun, though his surrounds was too dark for his eyes to capture any shape or movement at that time, but he knew that if he stays a little longer, his sight would readjust to the dark.

Thomas learnt how to fight in the dark during tight situations such as this in the Operation Desert Storm in Afghanistan.

He held gun butt firmly with his fingers pressing precariously on the trigger as he swung his gun about and at the same time searching for the door "Mr. Faceless" had told him he would find. His hand felt the cold knob of the door as he groped. He turned the knob and it made an irritating click followed by a squeak as the wooden door opened.

Gently, he walked but a bit shaky, with a sense of guilt for loving money more than his own life. The only source of light was a light bulb fastened to two naked wires that dangled loosely from the ceiling, reflecting over an object that suspiciously looked like a five-meter long golden casket with strange engraved drawings, which appeared to be scenes of a city on fire with people being burnt alive and dying grisly.

"What the…" He was stopped by a disemboweled groan from behind, sending shivers down his spine.

"I see that you failed me tom," said the voice behind him.

Thomas spun round in search of the voice, but to his utter bemusement, he met a tall figure rapped in a black hooded robe. His face hidden from view by the near darkness of the room and the overly dramatic huge hood.

Damn! This was not what he signed up for, Thomas thought. If he had not been confused about the information he was to hear, he was now.

"It's not as bad as it sounds," Thomas tried to explain.

He was good in taking in the pressure when it comes to clients, but this time it was different.

He knew stepping on his toe would not bring about anything good

"Do you have what was required of you?" Said faceless.

Thomas tried to place the accent. It was definitely not British; it was either American or Italian. He had never been good with placing accents or that sort of things.

Without realizing it, the figure had stepped closer to his personal space adding to the air of discomfort. Thomas did not like this one bit.

"It depends on your perspective," he was trying very hard to hide his tremor but he seemed to be reeling. He felt like he had lost control of his body movement, feeling paralyzed.

"I am listening," faceless said emphatically, "if you have what I need, say it now."

"My team and I had gotten a link, but we were prevented by some kind of a force and we were unable to retrieve any information," Thomas said.

He hated giving excuses to his clients, but he had lost three of his good men at once and it was going to hard replacing them.

"It's as if someone does not want us near whatever is behind the wall real bad." Faceless muttered.

Thomas could feel the cold eyes on him as he spoke. For a second he had glanced at his eyes, making him stumble backwards without even realizing it. There was something fearful and unnatural about his eyes. Something was not right here.

"But… but there was something I found though," Thomas replied and was now quivering.

The rope rippled, giving a sign that he wanted Thomas to continue talking.

"There was something about a girl though. I was able to hack into their system long enough to squeeze adequate information about her," Thomas said.

"May I ask how a girl comes into this?" faceless bellowed with anger.

"From what I figured out, it has everything to do with what you asked of me," Thomas finished, waiting breathlessly for a sign.

"And?" Faceless asked.

There was a hint of interest this time. This gave Thomas the confidence he had lacked since he had stepped into this building. "My sources confirmed this. Her name is Thalia Throne and that she lives in a secluded town with her parents. That's all I could gather, the dude seemed he had been scared shitless," Thomas said, and he just liked how he felt at this moment.

"Are you sure of this information?" Faceless asked.

"Positive," Thomas nodded; he could feel what he had been waiting for coming.

"Alavine," faceless called out, scaring Thomas, "Gason!"

A pale almost translucent girl appeared from my right wearing black from top to bottom; a black t-shirt that read-more like shouted out the word TOTAL RECALL. Black ripped up denim jeans, the only thing they could be useful for were to fill up the bin and not to forget the number of piercings that choked her face and in places Thomas never taught of seeing a piercing before now.

She could have easily fitted a 'wannabee' gothic rock star. She had on so much black makeup on her face that took away the last of the innocence that a teenage girl was to possess.

By his right, a man whose huge body would have put fear in the minds of any wrestler. The man was double of Thomas medium height and this hawk of thing did not seem crazy about his looks as the girl did. He wore plain jeans and a sweatshirt that did not do much to conceal the big man's muscles.

"Ha, my friends welcome," faceless greeted the new arrivals, turning his attention to Thomas, he spoke, "you have served your purpose well and for that you shall be rewarded"

Finally! Thomas though, he could get what he wanted and leave this freaky show. "I did love that," he said without hiding his enthusiasm. He stepped forward for the briefcase of money that he suspected would be with one of the goons.

The robed figure laughed but was not what Thomas would call friendly and this sent wariness through his body.

As Thomas waited uncomfortably fixed in a spot, he thought he heard a voice say, "the gift of death" but before he could open his mouth to confirm if he truly heard the voice, he saw a blinding light heading him. The powerful blaze razed everything on its path as it finally consumed him in a flash. A pile of smoldering black ashes where he once stood; and his loud reverberating cry that echoed across the walls of the dim lighted room was all the trace that was left of Thomas.

The hooded figure turned his scowl at the two visitors; darkness seemed to be surrounding him and something that looked like raw fear flashed through their eyes.

"Find this so called girl, Thalia, and bring her to me...alive," he commanded as the casket glowed with unearthly light.

Chapter One

"Thalia," Aunt Hailey called out, her voice interfering with my sidetracked daydream after just reading two pages from an interesting historical romance novel. I was not the romantic type, not by a long run, but if the only romance I could afford where from novels who am I to do otherwise.

"Coming," I replied as I dropped the book on the table that served as a makeshift desk for aunt Hailey's small compartment of an office behind the shop. I hurried, moving as fast as I could through the corridor that connected the main building, which housed the shop.

"Yes," I squeaked, as I came to an abrupt stop and an almost unavoidable collide with a not too happy aunt Hailey

She had stepped aside just in time before an accident could occur.

"What are you doing out at the back instead of working?" she asked frantically, wearing a suspicious look on her face, which she seemed to wear when around me. I could say I was a charmer, but I could be lying.

"Studying," I replied without giving a thought, as I still tried to catch my breath. Let us just say I was a little bit out of shape.

She gave me an I-don't-believe-you stare, but sighed in resignation.

Aunt Hailey had what people called an elfish appearance, if you saw it that way. I thought more in the road of impish, but that was my opinion.

She was blonde, no, blonde was not it. It was more like wheat white color. Perfect straight white wheat. She maintained it at shoulder length, but her hair had not been that length back then when her hair had reached her butt until she met her soul mate, Nate, a full-blown hippie and a raging sensitivity that rubbed on my aunt after much resistance. Therefore, she did the hippie thing for a while before she cut hair and donated it to a health clinic that take care of cancer survivors

Her short hair only brought out her elfish feature; pointed ears, button nose, big eyes and her too cheerful grin that annoyed the hell out of me and she knew it. She was like those type of people that in the next twenty years they will still look like a twenty year old.

Though she was my relation, unfortunately, I had not inherited 'the look'. I was dark haired for one and the funny part was that it was not even brown, it was more like the color of mud and a lumpy tangled mess. Nothing could get through and honestly speaking, nothing could get out either. I did not have her green eyes, but more like grey and not the type that were smoky or mysterious but plain grays. I had hand full freckles unlike aunt Hailey's flawless skin.

The icing on the cake was that I always carried a grimace. At least that is what aunt Hailey always complained. She said I was on old soul in a young girl's body. Maybe she was right because I have not been myself since my best friend left me high and dry for a trip to Scotland with her family.

"I really don't care about your teenage problem but I am going to blow a fuse if you don't serve table four right now," Aunt Hailey said pulling me out of my daydream once more.

"Sure," I said. I had enough energy to attend to at least two or three tables before I left for home.

"They need four cups of cappuccino, two milk shakes and five dough nuts," Aunt Hailey said. She was an expert when it came to being a waiter. Most of her jobs leaned on her experience with this kind of thing. Therefore, the families were not surprised when she planned with Nate to invest their honeymoon allowance on the diner. This was typical of aunt Hailey.

"One junk food coming up," I muttered under my breath. I took the order to Table 4. The only reason I was doing this job was that…! Actually, there was not any specific reason, at least not for the two years I had been working here, well, not until Sophie went on her vacation. Do not get me wrong, I had other friends but they were not Sophie.

"Hey! If it isn't Thalia, the loser queen," said a familiar voice as I got closer the table. Sitting round it were Britney and her goons: Jane, Kim, Lily, Carl and Billy.

Once in my 5th grade I had something going for Billy. Yeah! I am still wondering what they were putting in my cereal. Well, he found an out-going figure! Which meant the whole school knew too and they teased the hell out of me; it had been the worst term ever for me.

Now in high school, mature and all, I saw Billy in a completely new clear and shining light. Gosh. I cannot believe I thought he was cute. When I thought about it now, it leaves a fixed grim on my face.

"And if it isn't Britney, the Barbie never will be," I replied. She gave me a disgusted look.

Please spare me. Britney was like any pageant hunter, spotlight grabbing, drama queen you could imagine. Blonde bob, blue eyes, pouty lips, clear skin and let us not forget the stunning figure. Yes, she was a beauty, a stunner, but that was common, right? I mean I knew other schools that had the same rotten manners and good looks. So what made her so special?

"What are you doing here anyway?" She asked, with genuine curiosity.

"It's called a summer job, if you haven't noticed," I replied, trying not to poke her purported pretty face. Heck, how I hate her.

"Is this the best you could get?" She asked, looking around expectantly, as if she was envisaging the place to fall apart anytime soon.

"Better than yours, you mean," She said and the hidden snickers I got from Britney's goons fueled me on.

"I heard you wanted to work part time in the fashion agency down town, but they kicked you out," I said, pouting, to show just how sad I was for her.

Her goons could not help but laughed. They stopped abruptly when Britney stared at them. She might as well have them on collars and chains.

"You need anything else?" I asked, getting tired of seeing the bitchy face of her royal highness.

"Yeah, I need a can of Diet Coke; anything else would ruin my figure, "she responded with her phony British accent.

"Britney, the only thing you need to keep fit are those loose nuts up there, your so call brain," I said, "That's if you even have any," with that remark, I turned away and was leaving.

"So I could be like you, the losing unfashionable Thalia Throne," "Britney said.

Oh, no she did not. She had just broken the camel's back. I turned walked back to them, dropping my tray on their table with a dramatic bang, which attracted many stares. We will let them look; it was after all a free show.

"Britney you really should get alive," I said, looking at her with pity, and this was truly and sincerely so.

"I should say the same to you," She replied.

I was ready to punch her in the face when Aunt Hailey called me. It took me quite a moment to regain myself. Giving Britney a smile that could win an Oscar, I picked my tray and began to walk towards aunt Hailey. Just a few steps away, Billy started.

"Don't mind her; she's just a sore loser," he said.

"Yep! And you're Billy, the goat," I replied under my breath. I met Aunt Hailey in front of the counter. She was not looking too happy.

She was staring at me, hands crossed.

"What?" I asked guiltily.

"What was that all about?" She asked, she really sounded angry

"She started it," I said, not ready to explain myself.

"And you joined," she added her voice a bit peachy.

"But..." I began to argue but she cut me off.

"You could chase away a lot of customers with your behavior," Aunt Hailey pointed out.

"It's not my fault," I said, getting angry. Why was I to blame for someone else's stupidity

"I know it was not hundred percent your fault, but, you should have ignored her," Aunt Hailey said.

"I have been ignoring her, but right now she is on my nerve," I said, complaining.

Aunt Hailey sighed "Fine. Please find it in your heart to ignore her, this time for me,"

I stared at her. She had this fragile look on her face. I sighed. I had obviously lost the battle but definitely not the war.

"Fine, kill joy," I said, disappointedly.

"Good, what are you doing now?" She asked. "I have to serve that horrible group again," I replied.

"Leave that to me and you deal with the cash counter," Aunt Hailey said.

"Thanks," I replied. I sighed with relief.

I went behind the cash register, laying my head on the cool counter, seeking for relief from the oversize headache that over shadowed me and also imagining myself mercilessly punching little miss Britney in the face until her head rolls off like a bowling ball.

While brooding silently in my bitter juices, I felt someone take up the vacant bar stool opposite of me. Not really, into the mood for chitchat, I completely ignored and refused to turn to see who it was and hoping that my unfriendly gesture would send the message. Right now, I rather stick to my imaginations than face reality.

"If I hadn't seen it myself, I wouldn't have believed it," said the voice that sounded very familiar to my subconscious.

I raised my head reluctantly, mentally prepared to give the uninvited guest a piece of my mind. Surprisingly, whom I saw almost gave me a heart attack. No other than the only person who ever gets through to me, Sophie Andréa, the infamous best friend.

"No way," my eyes were bulging out of their sockets. Well I could not blame them, there was no way in Zeus's staff was I expecting Sophie, at least not now.

"Are you just going to stand there or are you coming to hug your bestie?" Sophie said using a slag commonly referring to best friend, with her signature eyebrow lift. She did not have to tell me twice. I made a sprint for her from across the counter that would make an Olympic athlete quite jealous and I would have been impressed myself but I was too busy hugging Sophie to the point of loss of air. When I was done, she was shocking and looked a bit red while I flushed with excitement by her side.

"Thalia I said hug me not murder me," she sputtered. I laughed. Sophie was something like a walking funny bone. Whenever she did it purposely or without realization, she always seemed to crack me up. It made her angry sometime but even with that it only made me laugh the more and that always got a death stare. You knew when to take her seriously and when not to take her seriously.

Another thing I loved about her was that she did not have straight hair, but curly waves and no matter how hard she worked on getting them straight they always went back to its normal curls. She was a red head which met her skin was somewhat pale but for some reason she really rocked it. She had grown over the years into a more matured looking sixteen year old. I always saw boys giving her the look, but Sophie always ignored them. Well most of the time. I had admirers too but they were not really my type.

"Sophie! I can't believe it," I said, giving her a look over. She was wearing her favorite Chanel boots over grey skinny and a soft sweatshirt from the feel of it. Sophie was good at covering herself because she got sun burned easily. Unlike her, I wore shorts and a t-shirt that read WORK HARD, PLAY HARD. My hair pulled up and because of the sun; I wore no makeup except if a lip balm counted as one.

"Believe it or not, it's me in body and soul," Sophie said.

"When did you arrive?" I asked, I was not much of a grinner, but right now, I could not stop myself from doing just that. "When you were giving that airhead what she deserved." She said smiling.

"I had to teach her a lesson sometime," I said, grinning satisfactorily. We gave ourselves high-fives; giggling. That was something else I did not do.

"I really missed you," I said, filled with emotions. I thought I was going to burst into tears of joy.

"Same here love," Sophie replied, also teary eyed "Why didn't you send me a text message that you were coming?" I asked.

"I wanted to give you a surprise," Happy that her plan had worked "When we traveled, things weren't the same - mum missed her yoga classes, dad missed his customers and I missed my best friend." She said, hugging me again.

I served her a chocolate milk shake and took a strawberry myself. She gave me this, am-I-suppose-to-pay, kind of look.

"No, it's on the house," I told her anticipatorily, rolling my eyes. Hey Sophie! Aunt Hailey exclaimed.

"What a surprise," Aunt Hailey said, giving Sophie a bear hug.

"Aunt Hailey, I missed you," Sophie said.

"Hmm... Aunt, can ... can I," I stammered, after what I had done I would be expecting her kindness.

"Sure! Take the rest of the day off," Aunt Hailey said, taking me by surprise "Come on lets go," Sophie said, pulling my hand.

"Just a moment, I need to grab something," I said, racing to the back room.

The book I had been reading earlier was still on the table exactly where I kept it. I picked it up, flung my jacket on my shoulder and hurried back to Sophie.

"I got surprise for you," Sophie said, as I appeared in front of her.

"Really?" I asked, I had not been expecting anything.

"Sure, you think I would have forgotten about you on that boring Island, right?" She asked jokingly.

"Yeah! But not when you were surrounded by all those hotties," I said, laughing aloud.

"Okay, guilty as charged," She said, picking up her drink.

"Whatever! But what is the surprise?" I demanded.

"It..." Sophie said, but interrupted by a pitch voice behind us.

"What a surprise!" Britney exclaimed. Surprisingly, there was a trace of genuine happiness and truth in her voice.

They hugged for a while as I stood at the background feeling a little jealous. Sophie and Britney had been best friends before I moved here. Sophie had been kind to me and that is when Britney had ended the relationship, she said she could not live with someone like me. Therefore, Sophie officially became my best friend that did not mean she had not on talking terms with Britney.

"So, when did you come back?" Britney asked. "Yesterday," Sophie replied sweetly.

"We should throw you a party like old times but..." Britney said as she at me, making her point quite clear.

"You decided to stick to losers and that's in our No-No list," She added.

I could not take it anymore.

"A No-No list?" I asked in disbelief. "I knew you were an empty head, but never imagine it was such a big vacuum," I burst out laughing.

"I never knew your type of specie still existed, I thought they went extinct two million years ago," Kim joked, walking towards me.

"At first, I thought you did get your numbers wrong," I said casually. Britney stepped in.

"You are a big disgrace to the social world," She said with a brake in every word.

"You are indeed a disgrace to the human race," I replied my words were shaky, as if I was losing my confidence, which I was beginning to.

"Please!" Britney exclaimed, waving and swaying her hands dramatic.

From the corner of my eyes, I saw Sophie pull out something from her bag and consciously dropped it on the floor.

"Hypocrites," I muttered.

She backed away a little, leaving her goons behind.

The next thing I knew was that she was lying on the floor face down. Britney moaned, as she stood up, humiliated.

"My nose, it's broken," She said holding it carefully as if it was going to fall if she did not.

"No! My nails, they're broken," Britney stared at her four broken nails, horror on her face.

"Oh my! I am so sorry. What happened?" Sophie asked, standing up to help Britney.

Now, I stood confused. Sophie picked up something, a banana skin.

She winked at me as she trashed it into the bin. Did I mention she was the devil?

"Hmm! Britney I cannot stay, I have to go," Sophie explained as she turned to leave. I could not help my laughter. Sophie grabbed my hand once again.

We both walked out and immediately we got out of sight, Sophie started to laugh. I wanted to do the same thing, but I want to ask you a question first.

"Why did you do that?" I asked, "I just wanted to show her that her graceful body could also make mistakes," She replied, still laughing.

"And you did indeed," I added, joining her in laughing. "So what's the surprise?" I asked again, now anxious. When Sophie had surprises, she went all out.

"You will find out," She said as she got into her car.

"It's time you got out of that shell of yours and do something crazy this summer," Sophie said.

I laughed, but I did not know just how right Sophie was.

Chapter Two

Squash, squash sounds the mop as I cleaned up the pizza blob on the floor made by some kid from the birthday party celebration here at the dinner who had eaten more pizza than he should, and I was the only one suffering it alone. Go figure.

"Thalia? I need you back here," Aunt Hailey called in a scream.

"Coming," I answered, tossing the mop on the floor with pleasure.

"Could you please help me make a delivery of some patisserie?" Aunt Hailey asked; her puppy face set.

"Sure, but I have never delivered one to a customer before." I said, it was not my job to do deliveries.

"You just have to deliver, get it?" Aunt Hailey snarled.

"Just make sure you meet the customer, and you can say something like, "Order from the Space Demand and Patisserie, yah!" Aunt Hailey said.

I watched her as she showed off her crazy moonwalk with her half split mini skirt. There were some things never to be seen by the human eyes, I thought, feeling quite embarrassed.

"Okay, fine, I get it," I burst out laughing.

"Here," she said handing over to me a package that smelt like fresh bread.

"Deliver this to Mr. Harrison. You know where he lives. Do not ask for money, he has made payment in advance," she said.

"Okay I will. Let me go and get my bike," I said, heading for the back door.

"Not so fast young lady." Aunt Hailey interrupted me. "You're taking the van instead." She insisted.

"But..., but I do not know if that's a great idea," I stammered. "The last time I drove the van, it you know how it all ended up."

Any time I rode any vehicle, it had always been a disaster, period.

"I trust you," Aunt Hailey said. "Now get your little butt to work and you mustn't wreck my van," pointing a finger at my chest.

"Fine," I said, "don't say I didn't warn you.

I got the keys and went to the van, open the door and climbed in and started the engine. I pulled the van out of the car park in reverse onto the street without crashing it yet. Well, I guess that started out fine, at least for now, but within me I was panicking, not only was the van in danger but I also was in danger myself. Concentrate, I tried to tell myself, that is the first step in driving.

I had better get there fast or I will be in trouble with mum and dad - no, that is so wrong - step-dad I mean to say. It was because of him that my dad and mum divorced. Well, it was not totally his fault but I was blaming him anyway. My step-dad and I always fight, and that makes me sick and that is why I dislike him so much.

I parked in front of Mr. Harrison's gate, got out of the van with the patisserie in my hand. Mr. Harrison's house was; what was the word again? Yes, unusual, it was like something out of a 1642 movie. It was not huge like most of the houses in the neighborhood, but more like a cottage size house, in a vintage kind of way, but in a modern setting.

Rumors had it that when the developers had wanted to tear the house down, they had fallen severely ill and could not go through with it. Now Mr. Harrison was one of the most feared elders in town for being able to live in this mystery house and no one want to have anything to do with him and rather mind their own business.

"Wow! Am I sure, I am really in the right place?" I asked myself.

This place looked quite different. It is homier, and what was with the flowers? Mr. Harrison did not pass to me like someone who will have the time to nurse a garden of such elegance. In any case, I walked to the front of the house and pressed the doorbell. I listened to the bell rang as I waited for answer, but instead all I heard was my own breath in the dead silence the enveloped the house.

I pressed the bell a second time and again there was no answer. Maybe he is not home, I pondered. Just as I turned to leave, I caught a glimpse of movement behind the window. I had a change of mind and decided to return to the door. I reached for the knob and when I turned it, I felt something strange, it was more like a chilling sensation. Goodness, is it getting cold already in summer?

Weird, who hides from their own delivery? I heard a slight click at the knob, and the door swung open gently throwing warm air at my face. Strangely, it did not look like someone was at home.

"Somethinghe I do for family," I whispered to myself. I hope I was not going to get myself into trouble with the law for unauthorized access. Well, sometimes I break rules, but never like this.

I closed the door behind me and walked in cautiously. There was no one in sight and I dropped the patisserie on the kitchen table. If he was not coming out to receive it, then I might just as well go now. I am running late and I am going miss dinner if I do not hurry out of this place.

I was drawn in by the warmth and toasty feel of the room, like someone was in the house. I had never been inside Mr. Harrison's house before, but it was just as I had imagined it in my head. It was like an English breakfast room. There was a medium sized fireplace at the far corner of the room, but was not lit, which meant there was another furnace somewhere in the house.

The furniture were mostly homemade and there was a large crystal chandelier hanging precariously from the ceiling. There was no TV on sight but a pile of newspapers and magazines on the coffee table in the middle of a brightly coloured passion rug in the center of the room

"I love fresh bread in the evening," bellowed a strange voice coming from the other end of the room. I turned slowly, expecting to see Mr. Harrison.

"Hey, Mr. Harr...!" I started but stopped abruptly midway and so also did my heart.

Standing at the far corner of the dimly lighted living room, was not Mr. Harrison.

"Mr. Harrison is... is that you?" I stammered; I hope I am not seeing things.

"Mr. Harrison isn't here," the strange voice came again. Whoever it was stepped into the lighting, causing me to gasp and fall nauseous. Whatever this thing is, scared the day light out of me. Behind the dimly lit room was a shadowy figure with scaly skin, like a weather-beaten leatherwear. It..., I mean he, was half my height. He had hair growing from every part of his body in places where hair was not supposed to grow and ironically, he was bald. He looked messed up and twisted with nails that curved almost to a claw and his green eyes twitched?

"Okay then, I better leave." I said, trembling as I quickly turned to walk to the door. Was I dreaming or was I just panicky? Who was this dude? Could he be Mr. Harrison's long lost cousin with a rare disease? Very rare, I thought in disgust with many unanswered questions, as I looked the intruder over.

"Not so fast," the dwarf figure responded with a voice that was as rough and repulsive as his skin. "You haven't met my friends yet."

I paused for a moment, and as I turned to be sure, he was not pulling a joke on me; right there in front of my face I saw several identically looking figures like him taking positions in every corner of the room. It was either Mr. Harrison had invited many of his relatives with a rare disease or I was in the middle of something worse.

What I am seeing cannot be true, it must be a dream. Could it be the grape juice? I must have taken too much of it earlier, and it is beginning to make me see strange things.

The figures were now closing up on me and it was then I realized it was not a dream and everything I was experiencing now was real. I have just come face to face with a gang of zombies straight from the cemetery. What are they doing in Mr. Harrison's house? I have to come up with some escape plan now or else, things may get ugly.

"I did not know today was Halloween. I would have also worn my costume," I said, trying to crack a joke.

I did not sound convincing at all. Oh my God! I was doomed. This was why I never like going on errands. I started edging backward towards the door, but saw that one of the figures was already standing at the exit.

"There goes my only plan," I muttered to myself. Now I was beginning to sweat profusely. This was now a game of death or alive for me

One of them came close and with fright, I kicked it hard in the face and he burst into dust and disappeared?

He could not have disappeared, It is impossible like the rest of this horrible experience. Well, if using my 5th grade karate lessons was the only way to get out of this hellhole, so be it.

This situation has left me with no other choice, than to summon courage and fight my way out. Now they were just a few feet away from me, and getting dangerously close. Just then, a sudden cracking shrill voice broke the silence, and I felt something wet grip my shoulder. I could not get a clear look at what it was nor could I get a clear look at anything else.

I started blacking out as I felt a sharp pain, like shockwaves to the heart. It felt like I was shut, at least my step dad, Ryan would be happy about how things are turning out, I thought as my legs gave way and I slumped. My head was spinning and I felt like throwing up.

"Don't kill her. She has something we want," yelled one of them

The shock had stopped but I still felt weak and everywhere was in black and white. The scaly figures were saying something but I could not grab anything. Were they discussing where to bury me? I had to get out. I managed to lift myself to a sitting position; I did not have a chance to stand because that little movement had caught their attention.

There was something new in their expressions, they looked like they had just found a long lost buried treasure and strangely, they were looking right at me. I could feel tears forming in my eyes. So, this is it? I am not going to die in a stranger's house; especially not in the hands of thieves, who wanted to get rid of any trace of entry.

I closed my eyes, imagining of Sophie, mum and aunt Hailey. I was not going to tell them good-bye. Tears started dripping from my eyes. I tried to pull it back, but I could not. I am not going to show any signs of weakness now.

Just at that helpless moment when I thought all was lost, I heard the door open with a sudden bang that shook the entire house. Someone had stomped into the house. At that moment, I must have been a little unconscious, because, all I could hear was the groaning, shouting and things breaking round me. I was too weak to open my eyes as I lay on the cold floor helplessly looking for what I could grab to pull myself up. Apparently, it seemed help is here and I am going to live after all.

"This is definitely not how I wanted to end my life," I whimpered, shaking uncontrollably.

"Get up! Let us get out of here!" I heard the intruder yelling directly at me, and it was not Mr. Harrison, and it sounded like a much younger person.

I did not wait to be asked a second time. Sluggishly, I struggled to pull myself up but collapsed. I tried again a second time but this time I felt the firm grip of my helper's hands and he pull me off the floor and into his muscular arms. It was definitely not Mr. Harrison.

He got me out of the house and onto the grass where he laid me. "Who are you?" I could not see him well enough but I knew he was not a student from my school.

"Here," he said handing me a chocolate bar, which he had reached for in his back pocket, "I heard it helps."

"Thanks," I took hold of it, but it was hard to fit into my mouth as my hands were still shaking. He held my hand and guided it to my mouth.

"You are not one of them, are you?" I eyed him suspiciously as the taste of chocolate melted on my tongue. He gave me this weird look,

"I saved you didn't I?" He said.

"Sorry, still woozy," I lied. Now that I could see better, there were things I was beginning to like about him. For one his eyes, stormy gray dreamy eyes. I was not a fan of boy beauty, but you could still admire from afar, right? He parked well from the tightness of his t-shirt and broad chest from the feel I felt during the test drive. He had sandy colored hair but the reflection from the sun gave him highlights.

He looked large and this was just him kneeling beside me. If I had been Sophie I would be flirting by now, but I was not Sophie and I was not up for anything after that horrible experience. Speaking of horrible, I was supposed to be home for dinner by now.

I only managed to lift myself up by leaning on my rescuer's shoulder. I was right; he towered over me, which was good because I was awkwardly tall for a girl. Why did I just thought of that? I had lots of questions, yet no answers.

"Thanks a lot," I said in appreciation, rubbing my shoulder where I had been hit, I could still feel some pain, but there seem not to be any bruises. It is kind of weird, because with the sudden sharp pain, I thought a bullet had hit me.

"How did you know I was in trouble?" I asked absent-mindedly, dusting mud off from my jeans.

"I don't know," he said, looking confused, as he gazed at the house.

Now it was my turn to stare back at him.

"What do you mean by you don't know? I smelled something fishy and I did not like it.

"Guess it was instinct," he shrugged.

I looked into his eyes for traces of humor, but saw none.

"Do you know who those people were?" I asked, not convinced by his answer.

"Trolls, they were Trolls," he said. "We have to get out of here now," he asserted.

"Did you just say Trolls?" I asked. I think, I am still pretty knocked out.

I did not believe my ears.

"We have to leave now," he said, looking very concerned, which made me uncomfortable.

"You just said those that attacked me were trolls and you didn't see anything wrong with that?" I was beginning to sound hysterical.

"Do you know where Mr. Harrison is? What did they want from me?"

He shrugged, looking at me blankly, as if I was the one troubled here.

"Trolls are real and I can't answer that question about what they want from you. As for Mr. Harrison, he is fine. He's next door with some friends playing poker," the Stranger said.

I walked directly to him, looking straight into his eyes, great dreamy eyes.

"Who are you? Moreover, what do you mean by you cannot answer that?" I asked.

"My name is Mike, I live down the street." He said, pointing to the direction of his house, like that was going to clear my doubts.

"We have to get going," he repeated, as he began to walk out of the gate.

"Wait!" I held his wrist. One of the trolls said he wanted me alive, what exactly does that mean?" I asked.

"I can't tell you that here. Meet me at Block 25 down the road. I leave there with my parents," he said, as he turned and walked down the street, turning off round the corner and out of sight.

For a while, I kept staring into empty space, not believing what had just happened.

I got into the van, started the engine and drove off without looking back; hoping that no more trolls or whatever they are would show up. Recounting the events that just happened made me to tremble feverishly.

I pulled up at the store, stopped the engine, slam the door of the van and I walked into the store. Aunt Hailey was standing behind the counter. I hanged the keys to the van at the key rack and turned away.

"Goodbye!" I greeted, without looking her direction. Thank God that She did not notice me trembling. I quickly rushed out, climbed on my bike and pedaled off with speed.

Ryan, my Step-dad was out, mum was chatting with her friends in the living room. I walked quietly to my room. Changed into my most comfortable pajamas and slumped on the bed.

I tried to force a sleep, but could not. I was restless, recounting the incident over and again. I then made up my mind that I must meet this Mike of a fellow, or at least for the purpose of therapy.

"No, it's none of your business. You just have to face the reality and stop thinking it's all a bad dream," I said to myself.

Seconds later, my eyes became heavy; I started to doze and gradually drifted into a deep slumber.

Chapter Three

I woke up startled and breathing heavily as I sat in bed.

"Oh, thank God," I whispered, pressed my hands hard against my racing heart.

I have been dreaming again. Trolls, monsters and boys with really long blonde hair and flashing grey eyes. It appeared I made it all up. Another nightmare, that again, seemed to have gone with the mist.

When my vision cleared, I began to get off the bed, but a sharp pain in my shoulder slowed me down.

"Aargh! Why!" I groaned, rolling over to the side of the bed to look at the time from the clock on the side drawer. It is six o'clock.

"Why am I awake this early?" I wondered, normally I was a deep sleeper which meant you could not wake me up at this time even if you tried.

Well, I was not going to remain in bed because that would lead to more sleep, which then means more dreams. No way, I rubbed my palm over the goose bumps on my skin. I kept remembering the dreams, and imagined if they were real or not.

I flung the blankets off and forced myself out of the bed and I felt yet another sharp pain. I felt my left shoulder where I always had this black mark. I had it ever since I could remember. Right now, it was the source of my pain and it was as if someone had stabbed me there repeatedly.

I went to the bathroom and took my bath reluctantly. I dressed up and ran down the stairs to the dinning for breakfast.

"Good morning mum, Ryan," I greeted.

"Morning," they both responded in a chorus.

"I'm starving," Ryan complained, picking the newspaper from the table.

Mum loaded our plates with pancakes.

I spread additional syrup, chocolate syrup and icing sugar all over my pancake. What do you expect when I have a sweet tooth? "Aunt Hailey said you were complaining of aches. Are you okay now?" Mum asked, sounding a little worried.

"Yeah, sure I am just fine," I lied.

"You got a headache because of driving?" Ryan said, surprised.

"Yeah," I lied again. Aunt Hailey and her big mouth

"We were actually planning to get you a car for your birthday," mum said.

"Really?" I asked, surprised.

"Yeah, since," I cut in to prevent mum from finishing her comment. I knew where this was leading.

"Don't worry, it was actually nothing," I said, yet another lie.

"Okay!" Mum said sweetly.

I shook my head in disbelief. I knew she had just tricked me without me realizing it. I heard a rhythmic knock on the door that sounded familiar. I felt relief wash over me. Who else would be as preppy as that?

"I'll get it," I said, wanting to leave the too awkward room behind. I got up and ran for the door, pausing for a moment to adjust my sundress. I had managed to pull my hair into a ponytail, but after 30 minutes in this humidity, it is prune to get messy again. I forcefully opened the door dramatically.

"Surprise!" Sophie yelled, her hundred-watt smile almost giving me an impaired vision. I could remember, since we became friends a day when Sophie had ever reacted to a situation negatively.

"Sophie," I replied with a lower than 50 watt smile, "what are you doing here so early?" In her hand was a big leather bag. I narrowed my eyes at her suspiciously.

"What is wrong with my timing?" She gave me a mimicked puppy face.

"Nothing but…" I eyed the bag again. She finally noticed where my attention was.

"Oh, this old thing," she said with an innocent expression which always never had anything to do with the word innocent, "it's just a few makeup items I brought along," she made it sound like carrying a bag filled with makeup was normal.

"Why?" I stared at her bemusedly. From the moment I had opened the door I knew something was amiss. I hated makeup, like models hated fast food. I left that to Sophie, she was an ultimate makeup freak. Until now, I still wondered how we became friends because we were so different.

"So, are you going to let me burn out here or are you going to let me in?" She said. In fact she was stalling, which meant I was not going to like it much. I stepped aside, letting her in.

Sophie knew this house as well as she did hers. I was surprised since most of our childhood memories of her where here. She found her way towards the kitchen with all the confidence of a queen walking into her grandeur castle. I followed her behind, shaking my head in disbelief.

"Good morning Mrs. Throne," Sophie greeted my mum, who was handling the washing machine, with a cheer that seem to bring sunlight in the room, literally.

You see, mum hates it when people call her Mrs. Throne instead of Simmons. Sophie and I decided to play this game we like to call repel rebel, where we get to annoy my mum with the surname as many times as possible, but for some reason when Sophie does it, mum smiles, but when I do same, I get grounded.

This was the only weapon I had against her. I had not taking the name Simmons yet and I do not think that would ever happen, and it drives my mum crazy, which makes me happy. I might sound mean, but think about this; you have known your dad since you were born, normally.

My mum and dad fought and decide to breakup without consenting me, rough but it happened. For me, my mum crossed the line, when she got married to a total stranger a year later, especially without involving you. It is quite traumatizing. Now she expected me to get over it. That will happen when hell freezes over.

"So when did you come back?" Mum was asking Sophie; she had this expression on as if she was considering playing the old "switch game with Sophie and me.

The thought was not making me angry, rather I felt like laughing, more because she was so stuck with me.

"The day before yesterday," she replied, not before giving me her nailed-it look.

I gave her thumbs up then nodded as I ran upstairs to my room.

"Bye Mrs. Throne," Sophie gave a light wave and tried to hurry me upstairs, but not before reaching for my mountain pancakes. We got into my room, and locking it after us. Sophie plunged her bag onto the bed as if she had been waiting all along to get it off her hands. Today she held her hair back in a French plait, which brought out her stunning face and she was quite aware of that as she had this stride in her walk.

"So what's with the bag of makeup?" I tried to sound casual, when within me I was dying of curiosity.

Sophie looked blankly at me as if I had gone mad, "Duh, genus, this is for you."

"What did you just say?" I must be hearing things. Sophie knew how much I hated makeup.

"Yes make-up. You're going to have a makeover by yours truly," Sophie said.

"Wow! When you said you were going to change me, I didn't know you meant this kind of change," I replied with excitement.

"Well, now you know," she said.

"Ready, as in right now?" I asked. "But I don't think it's a good idea." Sophie made a puppy face, looking a little dejected.

"Come on, for me?" she asked.

I rolled my eyes, knowing I cannot escape.

"Fine, just this once, because I love you and I owe you this much," the things I do for friends.

Sophie sat on the bed and patiently unzipped the bag.

"I told you before that you need to express your true inner self," she said, "Thalia, the one that doesn't care if anyone insults her, provided you do not do it to her face. That is why I am here, to help you!"

"Ah!" I pulled her close and hugged her. She was truly more than just a friend was, even if she does show it in a very weird way, she always meant well.

"Come on," Sophie said breaking the emotional hug, "now I know how they feel in soaps," I said laughing.

She pointed to a chair by the study table.

"Take a sit," she said.

I took my seat without saying a word, looking at her expectantly. "Okay, what's your horoscope?" Sophie asked.

It took me a while before I responded.

"Pieces," I replied.

She dipped her hands into her bag, fondled a bit, as if searching through a heap and finally, she brought out a magazine and began to flip slowly through the pages.

"Here we are, finally," Sophie said and started reading:

"Mates - she is gorgeous, talented and so popular. Become her friend and some of her charms could rub off on you,"

"Did you hear that?" She asked.

"That's so unbelievable, they actually wrote that?" I asked in disbelief,

"Hmm!" She nodded with a satisfied grin, "let's continue."

"Dates - You both really like each other, but there's something coming between you... can you manage to sort it out?" Sophie said.

"Too bad, that one isn't going to happen." I said.

"Really?" Sophie asked, thoughtfully, "what makes you think so?"

"Because I have other more important things to do," I replied.

"Yeah, like what?" Sophie asked sarcastically,

I went quiet. I possibly could not share with Sophie about my un- imaginable experience with the Trolls. She would send me straight to a psychiatric home.

Sophie gave me an 'I have won' kind of look. "Looking great," Sophie began reading:

"This year, something unexpected is going to happen to you. You need to actualize the inner fighting spirit in your personality. Trend; Biker boots," Sophie said.

"So?" I asked.

"Hmm, firstly, your style. Something to bring out your game look," Sophie replied, looking at me thoughtfully.

I did not trust that light in her eyes.

"Sophie, I don't want to change my appearance," I said with panic, "you're not changing it, just taking it to the next level." Sophie replied, grinning from ear to ear.

It is needless to start an argument with Sophie, as she will always have her way.

Sophie pulled out a zebra stripped hair straitening iron from her bag, and with it, she rolled my dead black tangled hair, lifted and then dropped it defiantly. She paused, stared at the messy strands of hair and shook her head.

"What?" I asked her, a little disturbed.

She did not respond, but simply picked up the straitening iron and began to work.

While she did that, my mind drifted to yesterday. I was still making up my mind to go to Mike, whoever he was, for some answers. What if it was all a dream and none of the things ever happened?

Half an hour later, I was looking at my face in the mirror and I could not believe what I saw. If someone had said I will look this good, I would have laughed to that person.

"Oh-my-gosh!" I exclaimed as I saw my new appearance on the mirror.

My dread-locked hair no longer tangled, making me look like a circus lion. Now it was straight and glossy with little curls at the front of my face. I had a whole new look. I weaved it left and right, sank my hand into it. The impossible had become possible. I really liked it. No, scratch that. I loved it.

"Sophie, it's silky," I exclaimed, jumping up from the chair, giving her another bear hug.

"My hair has never been this silky," I said, "or this straight."

"Never challenge an expert" Sophie bragged.

"You truly are." I agreed, there was no other way to describe it.

Sophie brought out a pink leather book, marked something in it, and then closed it again.

"What was that?" I asked.

"Just marking my first achievement," She replied.

"Wait, you mean there's more?" I asked in disbelief. What else could there possibly be. I mean, my hair is straight now for crying aloud.

"Yes, shopping and we are running out of time." Sophie said.

"You must be kidding me, right?" I asked.

"I never do my work halfway," she said, grabbing me, "come let's go."

"What about lunch?" I asked her

"We will eat at your Aunt's place," Sophie said.

We hit the mall before it struck one O'clock. On our way, we stopped at Space Demand for a short lunch of hamburger and ice cream.

"You're only to choose dark colors and a few bright ones," Sophie announced as we got into the mall.

"So what exactly am I looking for?" I asked, sarcastically.

"I'm thinking shorts, jeans, cut-offs, skinnies, tank tops, t-shirts, skirts and maybe some leather jackets too. How does that sound?" Sophie asked.

"Cool," I replied, "what's our first stop?"

"Unique? I hear they have the coolest things," Sophie asked.

"Good call!" I said, as we descended on the shop.

I promised myself that I was not going to think of my problems, I was going to have as much fun as possible.

Much later, both of us had an armful of flirty skirts or skinnies. We dashed into the changing room and started modeling the skirts for each other.

"Sophie, I love that!" I squealed, checking out her knee-length poker-dotted skirt with lacy hem. "It's fabulous."

"Thanks!" Sophie replied.

"But yours is over the top," glancing admiringly at my dark-pink sleeveless top with a ribbon tie, paired with dark skinnies. "It's pretty," she added.

I was proud of myself. I truly was not good with fashion. I knew that and just like makeup, I am useless in this department. We went back to the cubicle. I came out again, this time wearing black skinnies with hot pink tank top with Rhine's bones studding the neckline.

Sophie was wearing a pink flower-print skirt.

"You look godly cute?" I gasped slathering.

We changed back into our own clothes, paid for our purchases, then headed for the tops to find some hip tanks.

"Dibs," I yelled, pointing at a black tank top that reads, "my world rocks."

"Too cool," Sophie agreed, snagging a simple, petal pink sleeves shirt.

After two more shops and two hours of digging into clothes and accessories, we were good to go.

"See! You look brighter than the last time I saw you," Sophie said.

"Really?" I asked. She was right, I actually felt happier.

"I couldn't do it without you," I told her.

We walked to the park and immediately we approached Sophie's car; I began to feel dizzy, which was strange because I was never a fainter. My surrounding was going blurred and I feel like throwing up. I had that feeling again that I was going to die. I could not get Sophie's attention as she was loading the shopping bags into the boot; I had lost control of my limbs. I swallowed by darkness.

"Thalia! Thalia!!" I could hear Sophie calling out to me from a distance.

My eyes were blurry; there was a kind of heat inside my body. I could feel every muscle, tendon and nerve cell as if it is about to explode.

"Thalia come to me," I heard a voice calling faintly. I did not see a face, but I could see a pair of yellow piercing eyeballs in the dense cloud of darkness.

"Thalia," Sophie yelled. I could only hear her faintly.

She held me at my shoulders, shaking me until I groaned from pain.

"Thalia come on," the voice called again.

This time the voice had faded out even more. I tried to sit up, but went down again. What was happening to me?

Sophie helped me up, allowing me to lean on her.

"Thalia are you okay?" She asked, panicking, "you blacked out all of a sudden."

"Yeah I'm okay," I managed to respond, still feeling weak inside and my heart was throbbing.

Sophie helped me into the car. She drove in silence, which was unlike her. I knew Sophie was not talking because she is still in shock and it was my entire fault. She parked in front of her house and helped me out of the car, still supporting me as we walked into the house.

Chapter Four

Sophie pulled a chair by the kitchen table and guided me into it.

My head was still aching and my heart was awfully racing. The strange voice was still echoing in my head. Nothing really registered at what just happened.

"What can I get you?" She asked.

"I'm really okay," I replied.

Unknowingly, I touched my hair. It was still silky but a bit sticky. A horrifying thought crossed my mind. What if there is a link to yesterday? If Sophie knew what was happening to me, she would have joined Britney in brazing my own personal hell.

No, she did not have to know, even if she does, she was not as bitchy as Britney.

Sophie headed to the fridge and started pulling stuffs out. She peeled an orange and put the sediments into the blender with some pineapple, vanilla yogurt and apple juice. Then she pulled a pack of almonds out of the cabinet, put a handful on the chopping board, grabbed a knife and started chopping. She tossed them into the blender, and then turned it on.

"Thanks!" I said when Sophie put a frosty smoothie in front of me.

She sat down across from me with a smoothie of her own, and set a plate of cookies between us.

"I heard that chocolate reduces stress," she said.

"Works for me," I replied and picked up a cookie.

"Are you okay now?" Sophie asked.

"I am fine, don't worry about me," I reaffirmed.

"Oh really my friend?" She asked.

"You slumped, passed out and you say I shouldn't be worried. It could happen to anyone you know," Sophie snarled.

"So tell me, what happened, because I'm not going to believe that you actually, "shopped till you drop," she said jokingly.

I laughed and the tension in the room began to fade. "So, are you going to tell me?" Sophie insisted.

"Tell you what?" I intruded hastily.

"Why you fell." She said. "You must have fallen for a reason."

My stomach twisted. I could not possibly tell her what happened at the car park. It was terrifying even remembering it. The voices I heard still sends shivers down my spine.

"I... I do not know. I just felt weak," I stuttered.

"Thalia, no matter how hard you try, you can't lie to me," Sophie emphasized.

She deserved to know what in God's name was happening to me and right now, I do need a friend I can talk with. If I have no one to talk to, I might just explode or worse still, go crazy.

"It... It started yesterday, Sophie," I stammered.

I tried to take a sip of my smoothie, but when I picked up the glass, I realized that my hands were trembling.

Sophie reached out, took the glass from me and kept it on the table.

She wrapped her warm fingers around my trembling hands.

"I shouldn't make you talk about it, but I am sure something is definitely wrong and I want to know exactly what that is," Sophie said.

I sighed, took a deep breath and I told her everything that had happened the day before. About the trolls, Mike, the parting words, the sharp pain from my shoulder and the present scene. When I finished Sophie was out of breath, as she looked at me with shock and surprise. That was not the reaction I expected, sadly so.

"It can't be true," Sophie said.

"I knew you won't believe me," I said.

"I do, just... Wow!" She exclaimed.

"I wish I share your sentiment," I sighed

"So you haven't gone to see him yet?" Sophie asked

"Who?" I replied, pretentiously.

"Mike of course, he may have the answers," she said.

"How are you sure? It might have all been a dream. A bad dream." I said trembling.

"Really? I am sure you do not believe in that theory. Something might be wrong out there, something as dangerous as the trolls, meant only to be in fairy tales, are now walking the streets in this side of the earth?" Sophie lamented.

"Well, that is not my business," I pointed out.

"I see! That's why all these things are happening to you," she said.

I did not utter a word, so Sophie continued.

"Thalia, you might not be the person you think you are, but you need answers or else, you will go crazy," Sophie said.

I wanted to cry but tears would not just come. It felt like my soul was dying.

"So what do we do?" I asked.

"We visit your friend Mike!" Sophie replied.

"No way!" I exclaimed. I was shaking, too much was going on and I did not want to compound issues.

"Thalia, come on, please," Sophie pleaded. It is for your own good as well as mine.

"Fine, but on one condition!" I argued.

"What?" Sophie asked.

"If what he says make no sense, I will leave," I said. Pointing my index finger at her face.

"Fine with me," she said, swatting my finger away.

I finished taking my smoothie, thinking the conversation was over. I had the feeling that this was going to be a bad idea.

Sophie was the first to break the silence.

"If I were in your shoes, I would not have done anything close to what you did. I would bury myself in my bed with a bowl of chocolate ice cream by my side. It's my own way to commit suicide," she said, trying to lift up my spirit. However, the joke was not working and it was only making me to be more depressed, though I tried not to show it.

I smiled. It was a good thing I told her. I cannot imagine life without confiding in Sophie. She was my guardian angel and best friend, almost like a sister.

Sophie had a way of making stress and tension like this to disappear with just a snap of the finger. Even if my summer was not the way I planned, it made no difference as long as Sophie was here.

Chapter Five

Sophie decided for us to walk down Block Twenty-five instead of driving. It was not very far and it would do us good, both physically and mentally.

"I think it's here," Sophie said, as we stopped in front of a creamy painted house.

If I may borrow words from Sophie's diction, I would say, "The house was cute in a story book kind of way."

It had a swing bench on the front pouch and beautiful flowers I could not identify.

We walked towards the door and stood there for some time. Maybe it was a bad idea, I thought. Turning around, I waved Sophie good-bye and was about to go down the stair, when Sophie dragged me back.

"Thalia, you have to knock on the door," Sophie said, her voice laced with annoyance.

"No, why don't you do it?" I asked.

"Since you seem more excited about this than I am," she replied.

This reminded me of when Sophie and I were just six and it was Halloween. We had argued for almost an hour on who would ring Miss Stevenson's doorbell. That woman was scary. It was rumoured that she had never seen day light. Well, on that day, Sophie and I learn that the hard way.

Sophie seemed to remember this too, because, she smiled, shivered and then walked to the door and knocked.

Mike opened the door, with the door chain on and he peered through the small opening. His eyes seemed to brighten when he noticed who had come to visit. For someone who made it clear to come to him, he was a awful lot surprised to see me.

"Hi!" I said nervously. An unfamiliar look written all over his face.

The door swung open and there he was in full view. His hair seemed to have grown longer and the colour brighter. It could not be true that I am seeing this or could it be that I was too scared to face the task.

"You came? I thought you wouldn't," he said with a husky voice that almost threw me off guide. Almost.

"Here I am," I said. Gosh! I hope I was not blushing like a fool. I do not think I had ever been this nervous.

He invited us in. The house was a beautiful piece of construction, decorated mostly with marble and the furniture was either grey, black, brown or navy blue.

"Nice house," I said, admiring the beautifully set living room.

"Thanks, I would pass that to my mum," he said with a smile, "who is your friend?" He asked looking at Sophie.

"This is Sophie, my best friend, she just returned from Scotland," I said.

Sophie, this is Mike, the guy I told you about," I said breathlessly.

"Nice to meet you," Mike said as they shook hands.

"Please sit," I said as we sat on a furred sofa, which was warm and comfortable.

"You want anything?" He asked.

"No, thank you," I responded.

"I don't get why I had to drag you here before you finally said yes." Sophie whispered at my side, "he is so cute."

I turned to her with a warning look, but it was obvious Mike must have heard, because he was now smiling.

"She knows?" He asked me.

"Every single detail," Sophie answered before I could.

"Yeah, everything, even what happened today," I blurted out without thinking.

"What happened today?" He asked, looking a bit scared.

"Hmm! Nothing, nothing at all," I blabbed.

"She fainted. Well, not that she really faint as such, she just blanked out because she heard voices. She almost gave me a heart attack. It was scary." Sophie explained.

I turned tomato red on the cheek when he faced me, concern written all over his face.

"It was nothing, really," I said.

"What happened?" He said gently, and I decided to speak.

"I fell and everything began to blur and I started hearing voices and see things. I could not move or talk, Sophie shook me before I came off the trance. That's all, nothing to panic about," I assured.

"What did you see?" Sophie asked.

"I saw nothing except darkness," I replied without thinking.

"What did you hear?" Mike probed.

"A voice calling to me. It sounded shrill, like it was in pain and suffering or something," I began to shudder.

"Anything else?" He asked.

"Yes!" This morning I felt pain on my left shoulder where they had hit me with an object," I said.

"I told her she must have been dreaming, because birthmarks don't hurt." Sophie said, cutting into our discussion.

"That's no ordinary birth mark Sophie. It's a connection mark," Mike said.

I stared blankly at him.

"Perhaps I should start from the beginning," Mike continued.

"There was once a tribe of warriors who fought in an historic battle that brought peace to the land. These two warriors were best friends and they were strong, trustworthy and the greatest followers of a Great War lord Odin-Gail," he narrated.

"Wait a second, did you just say Odin?" I asked.

"Yeah, he is the god of war," Mike responded.

"Now this is beginning to sound like the stories grand mum used to tell me - trolls, gods, and then what more? Fairies," I said in anger, standing up.

Sophie pulled me down.

"Would you stop acting like a child and listen to him," she advised.

"Fine!" I said angrily.

"Please continue," Sophie pleaded.

"Gail, the youngest became over ambitious. He wanted to be the one to rule the warriors. Kauff, the older one had seen it coming.

"Gail challenged Kauff to a fight. Kauff could not refuse. Gail knew he was going to die, so he created a demon, twelve feet tall, or even more. It was to destroy Kauff and every single warrior if he Gail to fails.

"The demon was woken by the cry of his dying master. The demon killed fifty percent of the strongest of the warriors. Odin saw this disaster, and he gave Kauff the power to kill Gail. However, the demon was too powerful for me to eliminate or even coming close to that. Kauff only had the strength to trap it in a place where it couldn't escape," Mike paused.

"What happened to Kauff?" Sophie asked.

"He died," Mike answered.

"So that was the end?" I asked.

Though I was interested, I did not believe him. It was ridiculous and Sophie's wild interest surprised me.

"No that was the beginning," Mike answered.

"What happened?" Sophie asked, almost jumping off the chair.

"Trapped in the deep well covered with heavy rocks and he was unable to escape. For many years the demon was forgotten until one day when an old weary stranger walked into the town where he found the well.

"Thirst for water, he mustered all his strength to removed one by one, the rocks that had trapped this dreaded century old demon in the well, unknown to him that his action would free the demon and unleash upon himself the wrought that took his life instantly.

"The demon destroyed every single thing that crossed its path. Aldor the new commander of the warrior's tribe, called to his god to give him the power he needed to defeat the demon and he had his wish granted. He was young, strong, and fierce in battle. He defeated the demon, but did not kill it. Aldor kept its body somewhere where nobody could release it.

"Tartarus," Mike continued, calling the demon by its name.

"So the demon didn't die?" Sophie asked, her eyes opened wide with fright.

"No!" Mike replied.

"So what happened to it?" I asked, though not expecting a reasonable answer.

"It went into hibernation," Mike answered.

"Did it shut down like a robot or you mean it crashed?" I reaffirmed.

"Shut down, just went into a trance," Mike said.

Sophie tried to hold back herself, but couldn't as she now started shivering.

"Would you like something to drink?" Mike asked.

"Sure." Sophie answered.

"I'll be right back," Mike said as he walked out of the room to the kitchen.

"It sounds more like a story than something that really happened," Sophie said.

"You think so?" I said sarcastically, I thought you wanted answers.

"Yes, but not fairy tales," Sophie said, "do you have any other explanation for all these?"

She had a point there. I could do anything but listen.

"Phew!" I sighed.

Mike came back with three milk shakes. He put the three glasses on the lower weak table in front of Sophie and myself. When he sat down, Sophie stepped in promptly.

"So did anything happen next?" She asked.

"Yes, that comes to the part that answers your question, Thalia," Sophie said.

I shifted a little and inside me, I did not want to know.

"Go on," I said.

"After the demon, who was then called the dark one was kept in Tartarus, Aldor kept the key that would bring back the dark one into mortal world, where no one except him couldn't find it," Mike said.

"Do you know what it looks like?" I asked. "You mean who?" Mike corrected.

Sophie and I sat there, stunned.

"It's a person?" Sophie asked.

"Aldor also made sure the unknown person were protected and guided when he or she was in a confused state, so he signed up a protector," Mike said.

"Do you know who this protector is?" I asked.

"Matthew, a dying second-in-command told his commander that his great grandson would be fit for the role. And at his death, his wish came true," Mike said.

"So, who is the protector?" I asked again.

Mike fixed his gaze on both of us as he answered. "Matthew was my great grand-father," He said.

I gasped, Sophie almost choked on her milk shake.

"You are a protector?" I asked in disbelief.

He nodded ino acknowledgement.

There was a moment of silence in the room. Sophie finally broke the silence.

"Then who is the key?" Sophie asked.

This time Mike stared at only me, eyes filled with concern and pity.

"You," he said softly.

"It's you, Thalia," Sophie said.

Chapter Six

It was either time had stopped or my heartbeat had seized. Sophie held my hand and squeezed it tightly.

"I know this would come as a shock to you. However, it was best you know," Mike insisted.

"I don't understand. Why they would want to choose Thalia?" She can't even hurt a fly, well except bitchy ones." Sophie said.

"I'm still puzzled by that myself, "Mike replied.

Could it be true? Could I really be the key? My mind went through all the events of the past few days, and I started to shiver. Sophie held me tighter.

"What makes you think she is the one? You said no one knew who it was, not even the commander," Sophie asked.

"That brings me to Thalia's last question. At the time when the trolls attacked Thalia, she unconsciously connected with me through her birthmark. We're remotely connected together in somehow, just like one in tow or like a sword and its sheath." Mike said.

I sat more squarely. At last, I found my voice.

"But, but how did the trolls know who I am?" I said, whimpering.

"Somehow it leaked. I do not know how it did, but something tells me that the dark days are near," Mike said.

I stood up immediately, and saw Mike was by my side.

"I think you should rest a little," he continued.

"It's okay Mike. I just want to stand," I replied. He held my hand and barely felt his touch.

"You're flesh like any other person, Thalia," he said, squeezing his face for emphasis.

"Let no one tell you otherwise. I am afraid you must have it deep in your heart that you are different and special. Special because there is something about you Aldor trusted. Something neither good nor bad, just different," Mike emphasized.

I attempted to pull away, not so much to escape from him, but his words. However, I could not escape from my heart because he was right; I could not disturb myself because I was different. Being different or not, my name and person remains the same and not even the dark one can change that.

"Thanks," I said.

Sophie got up to hug me.

"You're still the silly girl I know. In fact you're not different," she whispered in my ears, "it's just for a purpose of why you are living that's different.

"You know you sound like my grand-mother," I said jokingly. Mike laughed.

"Ha ha ha! Very funny," Sophie said, "it's getting late, and I better go. I will come with you."

"No, I want to be alone," I replied.

"But..." Sophie tried to disagree.

"Sophie, she's right," Mike reaffirms.

"Fine, but be careful," she said with a smile.

"See you later," I said waving them goodbye.

I walked out, thankful that I had brought my jacket with me, because it was getting cold. My house was not that far, I could get home within the hour, that is, if I wanted to be fast. On the other hand, I could take the other way, which could be a long walk, but it will give me enough time to think, and that was all I needed right now.

However, I did not want to get home early anyway, so I walked slowly down the road.

The place always looks different in the evening. The fairy lights would be switched on which gives the neighbourhood a magical appearance.

My eyes stung as I fight back tears from dropping. I was not going to start crying, no I will not, chanting the words in my mind as I fasten my pace. May be following this route was a bad idea after all.

I stopped in front of the diner. The inside was dark, meaning that Aunt Hailey had closed for the day. Impulsively, I looked up to the sky, which was now becoming darker. If I get home late, I will just do a quick toast, I thought as I kept on the pace, but only stopped when I saw Mr. Harrison's house and my mind flashed back to the previous day.

Sights of movement at the back cut short my flashback. Curiosity sets in, and I tried to hold myself back, but I could not. Irresistibly, I tiptoed to the backyards, carefully so as not to make any noise.

I leaned on the wall, trying to blend in with the surrounding. What I saw surprised me. There were like seven or nine trolls. They just stood there tall and disfigured. I breathed slowly, trying to stay out of sight.

I turned back towards the front gate, before I could move; I heard two voices coming from the exact direction I was trying to escape through and I quickly looked around for a hiding place.

I dived behind a deck chairs and tables and ducked. Two trolls appeared. I noticed it was a girl with the longest strawberry blonde hair, palest and emotionless face I had ever seen. The second was a tall and huge man that looked like he could break anything at his reach. I kept silent as they came closer.

"Yes!" Said the Strawberry Blonde,

"He is getting stronger, but he still needs the girl, right?" Tally asked.

"Of course! Yes, he can't mutate to the mortal world without the key."

Answered Blonde.

Ice ran down my spine, knowing they were talking about me. "What about the boy the captain talked about?" Asked Strawberry Blonde.

"I heard he is to be eliminated and that is where we come along, and are they not after the girl yet?" Asked Tally

"The Dark Lord has other things to finish first," Blonde said, "so we crush anything that stops us from getting what we want," she continued with a loud laughter.

"I like it, I like to crush," Tally joined her, laughing even louder, sending echo into the air.

Out of fright, I moved backwards, hitting the legs of one of the chair. Strawberry blonde paused and turned around.

"Quiet! Did you hear that?" She asked.

"Yes!" Tally said in a gruffy voice, "right here."

Strawberry blonde walked swiftly towards where I was hiding. I held my breath as she came closer and closer.

"Me lady." Someone screeched, "I have found it."

Strawberry blonde and Tally's head swung in the direction of the momentary distraction. A third troll raced to the scene with crossed eyes, drooling nose and a lopsided mouth, and in his hands was a small black box.

"Let me see," sneered Strawberry Blonde, snatching the box from the mal-shaped troll. She lifted out two books with loose leaves like those that they were going to fall apart any moment soon.

Tally joined her as she glanced through the books, ignoring the troll. "One of them isn't the one we want." Strawberry blonde yelled as she threw the book at the troll.

"Show me where you got this one from," ordered the Tally.

The troll slowly walked round the corner followed by Strawberry blonde and Tally.

I slowly crawled out of my hiding. This was my only chance to escape. I walked to the front gate, and then paused; two trolls were standing on guard, darned.

Okay, for one thing, trolls were disfigured and stupid creatures, so they appear, but I was not sure how true that was, just that it is my only hope of escape.

I picked up a pebble.

"Please don't fail me now, please," I prayed and then threw the pebble at the troll with all my strength and luckily, it hit one of the trolls on the head, bingo!

I kept low as the act began.

"What did you hit me for?" Asked the first troll.

"No I did not," said the second.

The first troll picked up the pebble and threw it on the second troll's head.

"Hey!" The second troll bent to pick the pebble, but the first one did not allow him as he charged onto the other and a fight started.

"Another bingo!" I hailed.

Still lying low, I quickly walked to the gate and opened it slowly. When I was out of sight, I ran as fast as I could until my feet started hurting, but I would not stop running.

I was out of breath when I got home.

"Honey what happened?" Mum said as I walked in. I waited until I got my breath back before I replied.

"Nothing, Sophie and I were having great fun and forgot time was far spent. So I had to run home before it got dark," I lied.

I could not possibly tell them I was running away from trolls.

"That serves you right, you know," mum said mockingly.

"Yeah, I know. Where is Ryan?" I asked changing the subject.

"Oh, he went out, would not be back till later," she replied.

"Oh!" I exclaimed.

At least he would not be here to blast me with questions.

"Are you hungry?" Mum asked, as she looked me over.

"Hmm, no!" I replied.

"Just go up and freshen up," mum said.

"Thanks mum!" I greeted as I hurried away before she could respond. I just want to be alone.

When I got to my bed, I collapsed into it, banging a pile of clothes, which I had forgotten to rearrange. I stared unto the ceiling.

"What exactly just happened?" I asked no one in particular.

"I must be imagining things or am I going gaga? I wondered, hardly believing it was all real.

"What did they mean by The Dark Lord had other things to finish first?" I pondered, staring at the vacant ceiling.

"Did the person have other plans?" I asked myself, "and who was he anyway?"

I asked so many questions but provided no answers, all cleverly thought out. I was sure of it. These people knew exactly what they were doing.

I was not going to give up. It has just begun.

I was too tired and I have to go to work the next day. Seconds later, I went completely blanked, dozed off like a baby.

Chapter Seven

I woke up with a start, blinking quickly and the first sight was the empty but impressively laid out Plaster of Paris ceiling. I rolled over to the edge of the bed. I must have dosed off for about an hour or so. Rubbing my eyes, I looked round for the table clock. It was amongst the mess of mangled heap of clothes somewhere on the couch. I was still wearing the clothes from yesterday.

Yawning loudly, I dragged myself off the bed and stumbled to the window.

It was not dark anymore; I could see the bright morning sun towards the north. I was now completely awake.

I rushed down the stairs, glancing at the wall clock and the time was 8:29 a.m.

"Oh no! Aunt Hailey is going to be mad at me. "I moaned." The sound of movements from the kitchen started me out of my gloom.

That was strange. Mum and Ryan were not usually at home at this hour. I walked towards the door, quietly not sure of what exactly I was expecting. Adrenaline kicked in as I opened the door.

"Sophie!" I exclaimed, a little shocked, "Mike!" What are you guys doing here?"

Sophie rushed up and threw her arms round me.

"God! I was awfully worried about you," she cried out,

"I knew you were going through silent crisis. I thought you were going to try something stupid," Sophie said.

I stared at her, horrified as it dawned on me what she meant.

"I told her you had self-control and that you weren't stupid," Mike said, and by the way, you look awful."

Humour flashed through his eyes.

"Thanks a lot," I told him, sarcastically,

"And what are you doing here anyway?" I threw Sophie a questioning look.

"I told him to come," Sophie confessed.

"Did anything happen?" I asked Mike. I still felt weak from the whole terrifying drama. Thinking about it gave me the shivers.

"It's okay Thalia," Sophie consoled, "you don't have to panic. And yes, you don't look like fresh hell".

"I have to get to the diner," I said hurriedly, obviously not taking the advice about not panicking.

"Like this?" Sophie pointed out.

"Hell no!" I humped. This was useless.

"Why don't you freshen up, while I make you breakfast," Sophie said.

"But…" I began to argue.

"No buts," Sophie cut in.

I nodded to say thanks and headed upstairs.

Twenty minutes later, I was sitting on the dining table with Sophie and Mike having our breakfast eating.

"I really didn't know you could cook, Sophie," I mocked; I could not even imagine Sophie operating a dishwasher.

"That is an insult." Sophie said with mock hurt, "I could if I wanted to."

"You mean you didn't cook?" I asked.

"Nope, Mike did," Sophie replied, smiling knowingly.

I took a cursory look at Mike in a new light.

"You can cook," I said.

"Surprised?" He asked grinningly.

His golden hair seemed to glow brightly. I was close enough to reach out and touch his hair if I had wanted, but I could not because that would be weird.

I blushed furiously. What was wrong with me these days?

"It's not that I don't believe, just..." Something strange is happening to my head. I jerked backwards, my chair falling to the floor with a bang, and I used the table as support as I could not stand.

"What's it Thalia?" Sophie asked, getting up also and reaching out for me.

"I totally forgot to tell you guys." I said.

Mike frowned, and Sophie's eyes filled with worry.

"Tell us what?" Mike said.

He looking worried too. Somehow I warmed towards him. It felt like we knew each other longer than three days and it was beginning to scare me.

With a deep sigh, I told them everything that happened when I left Mike's house the night before, leaving Sophie and Mike breathless.

"But you never go pass Mr. Harrison's house, except..." Sophie said, as she stared at me with disapproval.

"I can never get anything past you, can I?" I asked.

"You are just one crazy chic you know," Sophie exclaimed.

"That's me for you," I said sarcastically, as Sophie rolled her eyes. I suddenly noticed that Mike had not commented yet. He had this look like when you finally find the last piece to a puzzle.

"Mike are you okay?" I said

I waited for him to reply.

"I don't think the trolls were waiting for you the first time you came across them," said Mike absent-mindedly.

Sophie and I had our attention completely fixed on him.

"What did you just say?" I asked not ready to accept what I thought I heard.

"Yeah, you heard me right," Mike said with a smile, as if what he just said had made complete sense. From what you just said, I think you caught them by surprise and not the other way round."

Sophie and I were still puzzled as we stared at him, blankly. Where was he heading with this? All of a sudden, my head started throbbing badly. I tried my best to drink my cocoa while it was still hot and drinkable.

"So you mean that they didn't know I was coming?" I asked trying to make sense out of all of this.

"Yep, I'm ninety-nine point eight percent sure," Mike said.

"What about the point two percent?" Sophie asked, as she sat back on her chair.

"The fact that they knew you were the one," Mike looked satisfied as if he had just cracked an important case.

"Wow! That makes me feel a lot better," I muttered, as I brought my chair upright and sat on it

"Let it out. It's going to do you good, trust me," Sophie said as she patted me on the back.

"Thanks". I said to her, smiling slowly," It makes more sense now, right? If they were actually waiting to ambush me, they would have, because I was surprised and the shock made me move. Even the strawberry freak said so or am I just confused and imagining again?

"I don't think you are confused, not in the least imagining," Mike assured.

I reclined a little, my thoughts whirling. We still had a chance. I still had a chance.

I stood up again, beginning to feel restless.

"So what do we do?" I asked pacing.

"The only thing we can do for now," Mike replied.

"And that is? Sophie asked.

"We have to know why they were at Mr. Harrison's house again?" He pointed out, "We have to search his house."

"Are you crazy?" Sophie yelled, her eyes bulging, "that's insane."

"But we have no other idea," Mike confronted us.

I took a deep breath. I had always heard that taking a deep breath and counting to forty is a good way to bring your temper under control. Only that I was already counting to ninety-eight and it did not seem to be working for me. Maybe, if I started all over, but this time slowly it might work.

I opened my eyes to notice Mike and Sophie staring at me.

"I really don't have ideas," I said sadly. I felt helpless. It was my fault they were in this mess.

"Thalia?" Sophie called, "did you hear what he said?"

"Yes, I did," I replied, and then glanced at Mike for assurance. "I'm sure he knows what he's doing."

"Yeah, I guess," Mike replied, smiling at me, and this made me feel special, which also made me annoyed with myself.

"What if we get caught?" Sophie asked, trying to be the rational one. I could not blame her; I was surprised at myself too.

"I would have that handled," Mike reassured.

"And what do you mean by that?" Sophie taunted.

Chapter Eight

I can't believe I let you convince me." Sophie complained as we sneaked towards Mr. Harrison's backyard without notice, though hopefully.

We got to the back door.

"So what do we do now?" I asked, my knees were hurting from the bending.

As an answer to my question, Mike brought out something from his pocket and dangled it in my face.

"A key?" I said, confused.

"Not just any key, it's the master key," Mike replied proudly, as he put the key into the keyhole.

There was a click and the door opened just a little. I pushed it wide open, slowly walked inside. Mike had not told us yet what he had done to get Mr. Harrison out of the way. He did not tell us, and I was beginning to suspect him.

The first thing I checked for when I got to the living room, seeing signs of last time's struggle, to my utmost surprise it looked clean without any traces whatsoever. Did not Mr. Harrison notice anything weird when he got home? The house looked like it was been arranged for a photo shoot or something. This was getting more confusing and frustrating as the day went by. I slipped out of my flip-flops to feel the softness of the rug. It felt like I was in cloud nine. I allowed my mind to drift to a happy place far from here. The sound of doors swung open brought me back to the present. Stepping away from the rug and slipping back to my flip-flops, I went to find the other.

I walked to the kitchen counter, and then laid my hands on the cold marble. Shivering as I remembered what happened.

"It's getting to you, isn't it?" Sophie said as she came behind me, resting her head on my shoulder.

"Hmm!" I nodded. It's changing my life."

"For good and bad reasons," Mike pointed out.

"Yeah!" I said with a nod. I lifted my hands from the marble, and then faced Mike with a sad smile.

"I suppose we have something to do?" Mike smiled right back,

"Sure," I replied, feeling warm on the inside.

"So?" Sophie prompted.

"From the information I gathered, for a fact, Mr. Harrison's study should be the last door down the corridor," Mike said.

I was supposed to be feeling suspicious at the fact that Mike had an information like that, from what little I knew about him I doubt Mr. Harrison occasionally invited him for a tea party.

We walked towards the door. Mike was the first to go in, disappearing into the room. We walked behind him, feeling a bit guilty; I would not like it either if someone was invading my privacy.

I heard Sophie gasp.

"I have never seen so much books owned by one man before." I said.

I rolled my eyes at her enthusiasm, though the study was a wow factor. It was austere and business like with a large desk, paneled windows facing the back fence with no great view to give the room a homey feel, yet sunlight still came into the room, freely.

There was three amazing ginger bread worked shelves and on it laid many books I doubt a library would have.

"I can't imagine Mr. Harrison being the reading type," I commented, walking towards the shelves."

"Never be fooled by appearance," Mike said.

I made invisible patterns on the binds as I searched through. An interesting book caught my attention. Slowly, I took out trying not to upset the order of the books. I looked behind to check if Mike and Sophie were also searching through the shelves.

I looked at the book, blinked, and then looked again. The aptness of the statement was what struck me. 'Ten ways to recognize a true Monster.' I read beneath my breath. Just below that, were the words written in bold letters. 'Monsters or Demons?' My head began to spin. I took five more books and went through them becoming more puzzled and confused.

I glanced at Sophie. She also seemed to be having the same problem. "Um-Mike?" I began. There is something here I do not understand.

"The book?" he asked, seemingly not surprised at the look of confusion on my face.

"I guess," I replied.

"I thought the same thing too," Mike said. Sophie came towards me.

"So what does this mean?" She asked hopelessly.

"It means that Mr. Harrison knows something about what we are dealing with," Mike answered, obviously confused too. "I think he knows a lot more than we do. These books here are not by coincidence."

"Mr. Harrison is somewhere near seventy-nine years of age," Sophie pointed out. "Isn't he supposed to be in the boring stage of life?"

"There is no way he could be dealing with demons," I said in disbelief, holding the desk as support.

"Mr. Harrison is fifty-two and just because he is old doesn't mean he does not have a past," Mike pointed out.

"It's just that it comes as a shock," Sophie said defensively.

"Sure!" Mike exclaimed.

Just then, I noticed that Mike was holding something in his left hand.

"What is that?" I asked, walking towards him.

Mike looked blank at first but then noticed where I fixed my gaze. "It's a book," he said.

"Can I see it?" I asked keenly.

"Certainly," he said, as he passed it on to me.

It was a book with plain black leather cover with bold golden inscription on it.

"Tales of lesser demons," I read, bemused. "And how is that going to be of help?"

"It definitely will." Mike replied.

"The question is, why they need a book in the first place," I thought aloud as I raised my hand to my chest, trying to make it slow down.

Just then, we heard the front door opened and then bang, it closed again. Someone was in the house

Mike tiptoed out of the room disappearing at the corner. Slowly, we followed him.

Mr. Harrison was on the phone by the kitchen counter. He was of average height, thin and had a grey hair, usually wore glasses and was not the talking type. He had a hard feature and bitter attitude. Right now, he seemed angry.

We hid behind one of the sofas as we waited for our escape ticket.

I knelt there listening to what Mr. Harrison was saying on the phone.

"Yes Barry, I get what you are saying," he said into the phone, and then there was a pause.

"A trick indeed, a very lazy attempt," he said.

"Oh! If I ever lay my hands on those scum bags," I said, standing fixated, trying to understand what he was saying.

I went round town to find that damn caller and right now, my back hurts. Immediately it struck me. I shot a glance at Mike.

"You tricked him. You..." I gulped.

Mike did not allow me to finish. He immediately put his hand on my mouth and his index finger on his lips, ordering me to keep quiet. Then he removed his hand from my mouth, but not without living a trace of his scent. Coffee and something woody

A faint pinging sound up deep in the house.

"I guess I'm needed in the kitchen," Mr. Harrison told the other person on the line.

He dropped the receiver, and then went into one of the rooms.

"Now," Mike signaled that we race towards the open door and escape.

We did not stop until we were two blocks away from the house, away from trouble.

I paused and risked a look behind me. The street was half-empty, nobody seemed to care that three teenagers were running on the street in the summer. We then stopped, to catch our breath.

"I cannot remember when I ran this fast," Sophie said.

"Yes, you have," I said, mocking breathlessly. "Remember when we tricked Angel into giving us her nicely baked pie on Fool's day, last year. We had to run for our dear lives and hide before she figured what had happened."

"Yeah, I remember clearly. I couldn't stop laughing all week," Sophie said

"Speaking of tricks, what exactly did you do?" I asked, narrowing my eyes suspiciously, as I turned towards Mike.

Mike went tomato red.

"Hmm... Nothing really," he said looking shy.

Sophie laughed at his change of color. I laughed too, and Mike joined in laughing as well. Our laughter did not last long though, as the events of the past few days got us pondering.

"I think it would be a great idea if we leave the street," Sophie suggested.

"You have a valid point there, Aunt Hailey's diner is just down the block, and can we go there?" I proposed.

"Sure!" Both Mike and Sophie agreed simultaneously.

Chapter Nine

"I can't believe you tricked Mr. Harrison into following you around town," Sophie pointed out as she, Mike and I walked through the glass door of the café, all tired and sweaty.

I led the way over to an empty table and slid into one of the chairs. Expectedly, all the tables and booths were occupied which means Aunt Hailey would have her hands full and suddenly, I felt guilty because I was supposed to be behind the counter, taking orders, mopping messed up floors and helping her restock the store. Instead, I was here trying to understand how suddenly my life had changed. I sighed, trying to clear my head.

"Bad thoughts?" Sophie asked not noticing my silence.

"Not really!" I exclaimed.

Just then, Sophie reached out and used her thumb to smoothen the crease that formed on my forehead.

"Stop worrying. It is not worth getting lines over.

"I laughed," I am not worrying Sophie, I'm just getting freaked out," I affirmed.

"Worrying or freaking out, as far as I know, they are both the same thing."

"Sophie is right you know," Mike said.

"I know, but what am I supposed to do?" I demanded.

"It beats me," Sophie replied, shrugging.

"The only thing we can do now is find out whatever his name is, is up to," Mike assured us.

"I can tell you one thing he is up to no good," Sophie commented, angrily.

"I'm with Sophie," I added.

"May I take your order?" Asked a shy familiar voice.

"Hey! Anna!" I greeted, happy to see a familiar face from school.

Annabeth Watchman was in the same homeroom that I was too. She has been a true friend to me since Sophie left for Scotland. I cherished her with my heart. She also helped Aunt Hailey after school and on summer breaks.

"Hey, Thalia!" Anna said. "Mrs. Hailey is really mad at you."

"I know where she is?" I replied, biting my fingers out of anxiety.

"She's out but would be back any minute soon," Anna said.

"Thanks for telling me," I said, as I sucked in some breath. At least I was safe for now.

She noticed Sophie.

"Hey Sophie, I heard you had cut your holiday short," Anna asked. Sophie nodded.

"That's nice," Anna said, grinning from ear to ear. "I missed you like hell."

"Me too," Sophie replied and there was an awkward silence. Not able to handle the gestured towards mike.

"Anna, this is Mike, he's quite new here," Sophie said.

Anna went red all over.

"Nice to meet you," She replied.

"Nice to meet you too," Mike said, smiling warmly.

Sophie and I tried hard not to laugh as we tried keeping a straight face, but not doing a great job at it.

Anna went from red to darker red.

"Anna I think something really very cold would do," I said.

"Ice-cream!" Sophie exclaimed.

"Three scoops," I added.

"No problem," Anna replied as she walked briskly towards the counter, almost running.

Sophie and I stared at Mike laughing.

"What?" He asked with such innocence, that we laughed harder and almost falling off our chairs.

"I think she likes you," Sophie finally said.

At first Mike went red, but then smiled mischievously. Then suddenly the doors into the café opened.

"Who's that?" I asked Sophie, who was directly facing the entrance. "It's Aunt Hailey," Sophie replied.

I glanced behind me and Aunt Hailey stood next to the counter.

"Oh no," I said, trying to hide my face so I would not be noticed. "Is she gone?" I asked Sophie.

"Not yet," she answered.

"Now?" I asked

"She went to the back," Sophie said, with a sigh of relief.

"Can I ask you a question?" Mike asked.

"Me, sure," I replied.

"Is Aunt Hailey really your aunt?" Mike asked.

"Definitely," I replied, "she is my mum's elder sister. She could be a pain in the butt sometimes though, but no one is perfect.

"Wow! I wish I had an Aunt Hailey," Mike said, with an exaggerated saddened look.

"You would regret saying that one day," Sophie teased.

I jerked as I felt something move on my thighs. My phone, I took it out of my jeans pocket.

"Sophie, it's a text message from your mum," I said, "she wants you, call her now!"

"I must have put my phone on vibrate," Sophie replied.

"Obviously," I said mockingly.

She got out her phone.

"Oh no," she cried out, "two missed calls."

"Maybe you should call your mum now," Mike suggested.

"You're right," she said standing up and rushing towards the toilet at the backside.

I wanted to close my eyes and chill, sleep or meditate and just flow with the breeze.

"Here's your order," Anna said appearing right in front of us. So much for chilling.

I choose the coconut chocolate chip.

"Thanks." I said.

"You're welcome," replied Anna, then she walked away.

Once the ice cream touched my tongue, it disappeared.

"Just what I needed," I said.

"I think what you need now is to go home and relax," Mike suggested.

"I hate to agree with you, but you are right," I accepted, yawning. But I have to wait for Sophie.

"Suit yourself," said Mike, "but I have to get home and do some translations."

With that, Mike stood up, dropping a five on the table, and then smiled at me.

"Until then, be careful. I do not think those things are going to stop and think over what they are doing. At the moment they have the upper hand," he said, then walked out of the café and Sophie walked towards me.

"Where is Mike going to?" She asked as Mike walked out of the Cafe.

"He said he wanted to make some translations on the paper I found," I replied.

"Good!" Sophie said absent-mindedly.

"Sophie what did your mum say?" I asked, trying to change the subject.

"Mum said I should come home in the next three minutes or else she will throw a fit," Sophie replied.

"You've a good reason to leave now. I have to go home too," I added.

"So, are you ready to go now?" Sophie asked, grabbing her ice cream.

"Sure!" I answered, as she led the way and we both walked out of the café.

Chapter Ten

I got home in two minutes, right before dinner, but mum was still on my case. We ate dinner silently, broken occasionally by a comment or two. I wanted to run upstairs to my room, but decided against it because, I needed an excuse, and I needed one now.

"Thalia!" mum called.

I raised my head away from my meal and looked straight at her.

"Yes?" I responded with a gulp.

"Aunt Hailey called," She began. Hmm! I could smell trouble coming.

"She said you've been missing work, is that true?" She asked, her eyes searching.

"It's nothing really," I lied. I could not have told her the truth.

"I knew you would say that," She replied with much pain.

Ryan stood behind the chair at the head of the table, listening quietly.

"What else do you want me to say?" I said, trying to calm her down.

"Why aren't you going to work?" She demanded.

"My life is a big wreck right now," I answered.

"Hormones are no excuse, Thalia," Mum pointed out.

"That's not what I meant," I snapped, "God, you don't understand what's going on with me."

"Fine!" she said, "what's going on?"

I groaned. I was not getting through to her.

"I'm going to call Aunt Hailey," I snapped as I stood up to walk out.

I had found my excuse, and quickly, I ran upstairs, threw myself flat on the bed.

I took out my phone from my pocket and dialed Aunt Hailey's number.

"It's me Thalia," I announced once she picked up the phone.

"Hey Thalia," your mum told you I called," Aunt Hailey asked softly.

"Yeah she told me, we even fought over it,"

"Oh. What happened?" She asked.

"She asked me why I wasn't going to the café anymore," I replied.

"And what did you say?" She said.

"I said I needed a break, but she didn't understand me," I replied.

"You should have told me you needed a break," Aunt Hailey reasoned,

"I wouldn't have called your mum if you had,"

I'm sorry," I said and meant it.

"It's okay honey," she said.

"So, can I come over tomorrow?" I demanded.

"Why not?" She said.

"You are my best niece, aren't you?" Aunt Hailey affirmed.

"Sure!" I answered.

"have to go. I'm having a piñata party," she said with glee.

"Cool, have fun," I replied, laughing at her childlike enthusiasm

"You too, I will try and call your mum. Is that okay?" She asked.

"Of course," I said.

"Bye!" Aunt Hailey replied.

"Bye!" I said, laughing.

When I hung up, I felt much better. I laid on the bed thinking over how I spent my summer. Sophie return, the trolls, my so-called destiny, meeting Mike, and out of all of these I treasured Sophie's meeting Mike more.

I had an old best friend and new friend in one week. It felt enchanting. Sleeping was the last thing I wanted to do, but I could not help it. There were important things to think of like how to get rid of the trolls, because right now they are winning.

Chapter Eleven

On Thursday, I went back to start part-time work again in Aunt Hailey's diner. Aunt Hailey kept her promise after all. She called mum and explained my reasons for not appearing during my shifts. She also made me apologize to mum for throwing a fit. Mum also apologized for being annoying and for not understanding. It has been two days now since our raid in Mr. Harrison's house. It is as if it had being forgotten because yesterday, I saw Mr. Harrison brooding over his untouched coffee, which was very unusual of him. He always paid, drank his coffee and left. It was like something serious had come up and it was distracting him. Something secret.

This morning, Sophie called to say she was not going to make it over to my place. She and her family were going out to do some shopping. The Jackson family always loved to spend big. Things were back to normal, at least. Mike had not shown up yet. It was as if he was ignoring us.

Therefore, I was surprised to see him at the diner as if nothing had happened. I did not want to go over to him immediately. I was not going to let him know how I hanged up on him and so I just watched him quietly from the spot on the floor where I was mopping.

Suddenly, he became aware I was watching him and his eyes lowered towards mine, smiling with an innocent boyish grin.

Trying to look casual, I got up and strolled across the crowded diner to where he was standing.

"Hey Mike! You have been avoiding us, "haven't you?" I asked straight to the point.

Mike's eyes went wide with surprise. "No, of course not," He replied defensively.

"Then why haven't we been seeing you?" I asked.

"I've been researching, like I promised," he said.

"So?" I asked, my heart skipping a few beats.

"Nothing much," he confessed.

My face fell.

"So much for hoping," I whispered, feeling a little out of breath.

"But..." he continued, "I have something which could help."

"And what exactly is it that you have?" I asked.

"I asked lots of questions and juggled to find answers to them. It is in one of such instance that I actually discovered that Mr. Harrison was formally called Dr. Fred Isaac Harrison." Mike continued.

He stopped to see my reaction.

"Mr. Harrison is a doctor?" I asked, my eyes going wide with disbelief.

"Yeah! Well, ex-doctor!" He replied, the excitement was clearly writing on his face.

How could I possibly be mad at him, I mean things had not been running smoothly since the beginning of the week, so why start now? I tried to kick out the strange feeling that comes over me each time I stay close to him. Managing to keep my expression at bay, I faced him, pasting a smile on my face.

"You lost me by your apologies," I said sweetly as we settled down at one of the tables far away from peering eyes.

He gave me a revealing smile. Well there goes the idea of trying to keep feelings out of the way.

"I'm sorry; I don't want my actions to seem as if I was abandoning you," he made the "you" sound more like a whisper and something more.

I was lost in his too gray eyes; I could practically see the tension. When the silence began to feel a little bit awkward, but saved, literally by the bell. My Aunt had a bell hung over the door to announce customers and since this was rush hour, the bell would be rung frequently today.

"So Mr. Harrison is or was a medical doctor?" I asked, trying to get back to business.

When I found out he was a doctor, I immediately went on the internet to search for doctors from 1545 until present date. In addition, I came across Dr. Fred Isaac Harrison. Dr. Harrison attended University of California School of Medicine." In his profile, there were comments that he was a brilliant, but not a serious-minded student of medicine." Mike continued.

"Why?" I asked.

"I will explain that later," he assured, "but first I also found out that he quitted his career as a medical doctor two years after he got his degree."

"Wow!" I exclaimed.

His last one year was a mystery. After that, the line continued on the part of his life. He became a mythologist, joined a group of other Mythologists, discovering artifacts and other archaeological relics.

Three years later, he went on his own and got into something that was dark and illegal. From what I heard, he stepped on some toes, and had to move from California to this part of town under a new name as Fred Isaac Harrison. The rest are his personal file." Mike narrated.

"I could never have imagined something like this could happen to Mr. Harrison. He seem simple," I said.

"Looks could be deceptive. Thalia," Mike said.

"Why did he quit his medical career?" I said.

"Mr. Harrison had always wanted to fulfill his dream as a Mythologist, but his father refused to listen to this. He wanted his son to become a doctor. Therefore, Mr. Harry studied medicine against his own will. But working two years in California General Hospital, his father died of shock and the opportunity came by for him to chase his dreams," he replied.

"Therefore, the reason he gave up his dream is never known?" I asked, still shocked from what I had just heard.

"I managed to get some more information. He was a friend to some Leonard Frankison. They were best of friends; however, Leonard started importing illegal drugs into the country, Harrison tried to stop him, but his childhood friend would not agree with him. They ended up arguing and they parted ways.

"They don't communicate with each other till they met again strangely, I don't know where though. Leonard was into something secret. He wanted Mr. Harrison to join him for old times' sake, but what Leonard was doing was dark and Mr. Harrison did not want to take part in it. Afraid that Leonard might kill him, he ran away." Mike paused. "What I found out about Leonard stopped me from searching more about Mr. Harrison, and I concentrated on Leonard."

What he said shocked me.

"And why is that?" I interrupted

"Because Leonard, also called The Dark Lord, is the evil one that wants to resurrect the fallen demon," Mike replied.

Chapter Twelve

Saturday came very slowly. Mum and I had started a housecleaning tradition every last Saturday of the month. It had always been fun for me a way to reconnect with my mum, but today I did not feel like coming out of my room or even doing anything.

However, it was the only tradition we kept after she hooked up with Ryan. I was not going to give him the satisfaction of finally ruining our fragile relationship. It was silly, yes, but it got us close together, not like mother and daughter, but like best friends, which was unusual around here since he came along.

I especially do not want Ryan to get suspicious and start nosing around. I hated him. Hated the fact that mum had confidence in him and that he was trying so hard to convince me into accepting him, but I promised that I would never accept him as my father, a step-father or anything else for that matter, except as a stranger who walked into my mother's life, trying to destroy it.

I felt sick all over as I cleaned the vintage blue sofa in the living room.

"Honey!" Mum called, breaking into my thoughts.

"Yes mum?" I replied, not looking up to see her face as she appeared from the kitchen into the living room.

"Please, could you take over from here?" she asked, she folded her gloved hands as she leaned by the door.

"I have cleaned the kitchen, the living room looks nice. I just need for you to do a little trimming on my rose garden." She said.

"Sure mum, but are you going somewhere?" I asked, hesitantly.

"Well...," she began and her voice a little shaky.

"Ryan is taking me out on a company dinner, and then we are going to St. Roman's Restaurant for a special treat," she added carefully, her eyes were bright from excitement.

"Enjoy yourself," I muttered, trying to sound happy for her, but it came out cold.

Not looking at her face to see her expression, I excused myself politely and went towards the garden in the backyard.

It took me thirty minutes to trim the rose garden, but I ended up with three splinters in my finger and a broken heart. I could not believe she stood me up for him without remorse. I sat on the barstool, found a little pair of tweezers from the kitchen drawer and carefully removed the splinters, groaning a little at the pain.

I got out a jug filled with ice-cubes, placing two cubes on the fingers.

"Thalia?" mum called.

"Not now." I groaned to myself, wanting to scream, but I held back.

I walked out of the kitchen into the living room and took a deep breath, and that is when I saw her wearing a silk halter grey dress with no sleeves with its long skirt looking flirtatiously on her. Her long black hair was loose and fallen down to her shoulder, making her look radiantly beautiful and younger than in her casual jeans and top.

"Wow! Mum," I felt speechless. Mum did a twirl in front of me, happiness was radiating from her, like the scent from a rose flower, which made me a bit guilty, yes, just a little bit.

"How do I look? She asked, smiling cheerfully.

I have never seen my mum look so pretty and satisfactory for a very long time.

"You look really beautiful, mum." I replied looking at her admirably.

"You look out of this world." Commented Ryan as he came down the Stairs."

"Thank you honey," Mum replied with a blush. I rolled my eyes in pure teenage disgust.

Ryan noticed me standing by the stairs.

"Thalia I hope you don't mind my stealing your mother for a few hours," he requested with a humorous twinkle in his eyes.

I groaned when he said the word "stealing," he was not only stealing her, but the happiness that we had both shared before he arrived.

"I would have loved for you to come with us, but I thought you would rather like to spend time with your friend, Sophie," he excused.

"I wouldn't come even if you asked me to," I answered without really thinking it over.

This is what I go through; he steals something from me and then gives an innocent excuse. There was an uncomfortable moment of silence in the house as I stared at Ryan with bitterness.

"Ryan, we are late already?" mum asked, breaking the tension.

"Yeah, you have a point," he said as he led the way towards the door, "have a nice day Thalia," he greeted, and with that he and mum left.

I could hear the engine roar and the car reversing into the street before zooming away.

"Phew!" I sighed.

I went upstairs to my room to do a bit of exercise to blow off some steam. I finished cleaning my room, and I was dead on my feet by the time I was done. I went down to get a cup of iced-tea, and then went to the bathroom to clean up.

I dressed in a pair of white cut-off jeans and dusty t-shirt and a pair of gladiator sandals. I decided to leave my hair down, straightening it a little with my new hair straightening iron Aunt Hailey got for me on my birthday. Since the day Sophie had done a miracle on my hair, it seemed to be behaving itself.

I lay on the sofa and turned on the TV, but I did not seem to notice what was going on, on the screen. I yawned, obviously fatigued from lack of sufficient sleep lately. I started to dose again as I can barely open my eyes. I feel asleep and immediately started having a nightmare.

When I woke up, I could not remember a thing about the dream and could feel a little chilly in my head. It felt like when someone invaded your space without you realizing, yet you just feeling that someone had been there.

While still pondering, I dosed off again and started dreaming. In my sleep, I could hear a buzzing sound coming from a distance not too far and felt something was crawling up my lap, but my eyelid were very heavy with sleep and couldn't open to see what was there.

The creepy sensation seemed to get worse on my lap which startled me out of my sleep and I woke up to find the TV was still turned on and loud. I must have slept on the TV remote accidentally pressed the volume button.

I was awake, yet I could still feel the strange crawling sensation on my hip. I looked down at my pocket and found the vibration of my phone caused the crawling sound. I got it out of my pocket, and Sophie's name boldly displayed on the screen.

I picked up the phone and pressed the answer button and lifting it to my ear, my hands clumsy.

"Sophie, what's up?" I asked.

"Nothing much really," Sophie replied, "I have been calling you like forever, what is happened?" She was sounding disturbed.

"I was taking a nap that's all," I replied.

"Sorry if I woke you up. I know you haven't been getting much sleep lately," she apologized.

"It's okay. I was already half awake anyways," I said.

"I just called to tell you that Mike wants to see us in the local library," she said.

"Why?" I asked.

"He didn't say. Just said I should call you and that both of us should come over to the library," she replied.

I moaned, struggling to come off my sleep.

"For the few days I have known Mike, he likes to keep his audience in suspense," Sophie said, noticing the worry in my voice.

"Me too," I replied, agreeing with her. "And when are we expected to arrive there?"

"Now!" She urged.

I looked at my watch.

"Sophie, its Five-thirty seven p.m." I said.

"I know it's late, but it's important," Sophie replied.

"Okay, I will be there shortly," I assured.

"See you, and be careful. Do not get into trouble. You know curiosity kills the cat. And please take the city bus, not that I'm saying walking isn't good though," she advised.

"I know, I will take a bus," I said, breaking her safety lectures. Ah! She almost sounded like my mum.

"Cha...Cha!" She said.

"Bye!" I replied.

There was a click on the other side, Sophie hanged up and

I put my phone back into my pocket, took my jacket, locked the main door of the house and ran over to the bus stop.

Chapter Thirteen

Twenty frustrating minutes later, I arrived at the library. It had been the town's first two-floor building since the early years of the founders. It was not grandiose or had anything special about it, but I loved it, though people hardly came here, except when they had to find a book from two centuries ago. That was how old the town and library were.

The reason for that was that, over the years everyone built their own library and would not need to come to an old-fashioned library that sometimes smelt as if it was a mold, and I heard rumours that ghosts haunted it. Thanks to the town for the renovation of the library and few people who wanted some adventure and an excuse to come face to face with ghost, visit it.

I met with Sophie at the entrance of the Library.

"Hey! Where is Mike?" I asked.

"He is inside, I just came out here to wait for you," Sophie replied.

"Has Mike told you anything," I asked.

"Nope, he said we should wait for you to come over first." She answered.

"Then, what are we waiting for?" I demanded.

We walked through the entrance. The whole ground floor was the library hall, while the top floor served as the Town hall, which used for Conferences.

"He's here somewhere," Sophie said.

We saw Mike sitting on one of the library reading tables. There was a mountain of books in front of him. It looked like he had been here awhile and was not getting much sleep either, from the looks of it.

We both hurried over to him.

"Hi Mike," I said when we got close to him

"Hey Thalia, sorry, I had to call you guys urgently," he said.

His highlights were more obvious under the reading lamps and so was the cut on his lip and black eye that became obvious by the luminous light.

"Mike, are you okay?" I asked, surprised at how concerned I was. I could feel fear rushing through me.

"Are you hurt?" Sophie asked, I gasped, and finally realizing what I saw.

Someone could have done that to him, I mean, He had fought a bunch of trolls the first day we had met without much trouble. Who could have done that?

"The trolls did this to you?" Sophie asked.

It had not been the question up till now. With the sudden realization, I could feel my eyes widen to the size of a baseball. He looked defeated.

"Yes and two other freaks," he sighed.

"This all happened today?" Sophie asked drawing a chair out for herself.

"No, it happened on Tuesday," he replied, looking guilty.

Well he should, for lying to us and keeping us in the dark.

"Why would they want to do that?" Sophie asked, bemused.

Mike was silent. Then it struck me, I remember what the huge guy had said that day in Mr. Harrison's back yard.

"I overheard them saying it was the part of the job to kill him," I said absent-mindedly, "I didn't understand what they meant then, I just thought it was none of my business then." I paused to see their reactions and they both seemed suddenly attentive, and there was this look on Mike's face that showed he already knew where this whole thing was headed.

"It seems that the 'him' they want to kill is you, Mike," Sophie said, looking horrified,

"Kill!" she exclaimed.

"You mean it's that serious? They can kill to get what they want. She seemed to try to convince herself otherwise.

"Yes, I heard the two freaks discussing it when they went to raid Mr. Harrison's house," I explained

"What happened?" Sophie asked, the question was directed at Mike.

"I was going to the café, so I decided to go through the park to spend some time. Before I knew it, I was surrounded by a bunch of ugly looking and disfigured trolls," Mike said.

"That is why you didn't show up?" I asked, "why didn't you tell us?"

Why do I have to make friends with someone so stubborn?

"I didn't want to scare you guys." he replied, looking at me nervously. I knew he could see the anger raging inside me

"But you still did." Sophie said dryly as if she was having the same thoughts I had.

"How did you manage to escape?" I asked, as my heart began to beat faster.

"The trolls might look intimidating but they are stupid creatures. I just had to mess with their heads and I took the chance to escape," Mike said.

His eyes looked bright. I did not know if it was from the reading lights or he was happy that he had finally gotten it out of his chest, whichever way, his eyes were beautiful and I felt drawn to it.

"But why would they want to kill you?" Sophie questioned. She looked scandalized.

"Because I'm the key's protector," he said factually.

"Oh! I forgot that one," Sophie smiled sheepishly.

"It's not safe for any one of us anymore," I said, as I stared at my friends, no one close to me was safe and it was my entire fault.

"Except for me," Sophie said, not noticing the weird exchange of looks Mike and I passed.

"You are Thalia's best friend. You have already become a weak link into trapping their prey," Mike said.

"Gee! Thanks," Sophie said rolling her eyes.

I really could not help but laugh, Sophie was good that way.

"Sorry, if I was harsh," Mike said, his eyes sparkling as he tried to hide his own outburst.

"It's okay, you're right, we aren't safe anymore," I confirmed, getting serious again.

"Then evil is surely winning," he said nodding.

He could not hide the sadness in his note.

"Not if we fight back," Sophie said, sounding more serious than I had ever heard her, and I mean ever.

"That's why I brought you guys here. As they say knowledge is power," he said with a smile that did not reach his eyes.

"Why are we here exactly?" I asked.

"This library has been here since this town came to existence, right?"

Mike said, using his fingers to comb through his hair.

"Yes, as long as I can remember," Sophie answered, chewing the gum she had brought out of her bag.

"This place could as well be like a museum for the town," Mike said.

"You've lost me." I replied, drawing out a chair out next to Sophie.

"Remember the story I told you about the best friends?" Mike asked, leaning close to us in a whisper to avid been heard.

"Yeah!" I said.

"That history happened in this very town. So if this place was built from the beginning…." he stopped, letting us figure out the rest.

"Our answers could be here," I added.

Mike nodded, enthusiastically.

"I think I'm seeing the library with new eyes," Sophie said, glancing at the shelves.

"Me too," I exclaimed, "how come I never thought of this?"

"I got some books from the shelves before you came," Mike said, pointing towards the pile of books in front of us.

"Wow! That's a lot," Sophie said, emphasizing on the lot.

That's why if we start now, we should be done in the evening," Mike assured.

"Sure enough," Sophie muttered, doubtful."

"Can we begin? I have to get home before nine o'clock," I said.

One tiresome, useless and wasteful heck of an hour later.

"I am stuck," Sophie said dropping the book she was trying her best to read.

"Me too," I agreed, my brain had gone book numb.

"We just wasted an hour of our time," Mike muttered with a yawn.

"Maybe we missed something," Sophie said, getting up from her seat. "I will go and check," she said, and disappeared through the maze of Shelves.

I dropped my book. Mum and Ryan must be enjoying their lovely dinner by now, I thought. Just then, I realized something. Mum never dressed that elegantly when step dad took her out. It hurts me to think mum dressed extra special for Ryan when she had never done that for dad.

"You're worried," Mike said, noticing the frown on my face. "Sorry!" I said, pinning a smile on my face, "I have issues with parents."

"I'm sorry to pry, but what kind of issues?" He asked.

"It is about my mum and her husband," I said with distaste.

"Are they fighting?" Mike asked.

"I wish, I have a problem with her husband," I replied, I could feel a chill run through my body.

"Isn't he your step-father?" He asked.

"No!" I said automatically without thinking.

However, I was never good at lying, though my stepfather is, unfortunately.

"Why do you hate him?" Mike asked.

"I don't hate him, I dislike him and I don't trust him, I'm sure he wants something from my mum," I said absent-mindedly.

"Why? Did he hurt you?" Mike asked, his voice laced with concern.

"No, it's just the way he barged into our lives, my mum and I, so suddenly. It makes me very suspicious," I said.

"I don't think you dislike him, because your mum remarried, but because he went between you and mum," Mike said, his grey eyes twinkling brighter.

"How are you so sure?" I taunted, regretting why I told him in the first place. I hardly told anybody how I felt about my mum's marriage, not even Sophie.

"Because I know how it feels," he answered.

"That was not the answer I expected," I stared at him, confused.

"My mum isn't really my mum, you know," he looked a bit sad as he said this, as if he was remembering something he did not like.

He met my searching gaze and sat leaning back on his chair, his grey eyes glittering faintly, while he waited with patience for me to put the final puzzle together.

My eyes widened with understanding. He chuckled at my wide-eyed stare.

"She's my step-mum. My biological mum died of blood cancer when I was three. My dad remarried two years back. It took me one year to get used to her," Mike explained, giving me a smile that did not really reached his eyes. When I did not respond, he continued.

"I had the same problem with her. My father and I always had fun together. We visited places. He was like the best friend I would ever have. Nevertheless, when he remarried, he hardly had time for me anymore. I began to make an enemy with someone who was not supposed to be one. It took me months to understand that I hadn't lost my best friend, the circle just grew bigger."

"It's not the same thing with me," I pointed out when I got my voice back.

"That's what I thought too," Mike responded

"He is not only stealing the happiness between my mum and myself, he is also up to something, " I told Mike with the anger I had been trying to hide for quite a long time now.

"Why do you think so?" Mike enquired, leaning forward, his breath teasing down my neck. It took me almost a minute to respond.

"Because I have the feeling I'm right," I said, not only to him, but to myself also.

"Thalia, sometimes our feelings are wrong," he seemed to be getting angry himself.

"That doesn't mean it can't be right," I said hotly. He had no right to take sides with my stepfather.

Mike was about to protest, but Sophie came over with a pile of books, dropping them with a loud thud on the table.

"Look what I found," she said gleefully, feeling proud of her self. I picked a book.

"Night in the Knight" I read it aloud, giving Sophie a puzzled look.

"It's supposed to be Knight in the Night," Sophie corrected.

"It's a confusing statement," I said, "I don't still get it."

"Night is something described as darkness. So, what is the actual meaning?" Sophie began.

"Darkness in the knight," Mike finished off with a smile

"I still don't get it," I said dropping the book back on the pile, replacing it with a black and gold book and started flipping through. Mike did the same thing.

"Suit yourself." Sophie said, picking up the "Knight in the Night and sat down on the chair opposite of me.

Fifty-two minutes later, I was about giving up when Sophie yelled.

"What was that for? I asked, covering my ears with my hands for their safety.

"Sorry I was just excited," she said.

"What for?" Mike asked, looking as lost as I felt at Sophie.

"Because I found something," Sophie said with a grin. She waved the knight in the night book. "Word of the Night or Knight, which ever you prefer, and Bingo! It's in English."

"Anything we can find out has to help, I said, "what does it say?"

"Um!" Sophie said," Um…"

The book began to rattle, and I realized that Sophie's hands were shaking. Mike leaned closer to Sophie and tilted his head, trying to read what had gotten her so freaked. Mike read silently, his eyes growing wide now.

"What?" I asked, I was beginning to freak out.

Mike's huge eyes met mine, but he did not speak. I took the book from Sophie's stiffened hands and began to read aloud.

"The word of the knight. When the moon is full, the ritual would proceed, because that is when the stone is more powerful and the one who bears this burden shall be stripped of body, soul and blood as only this can bring the dead to life. This ritual cannot be complete without the stone of mysterious power. And then the Knight in the Night shall rise." It read.

Then I understood why Sophie and Mike were agitated out now.

"The Knight in the Night means Gail's demon, created almost by his own image," Mike said, getting his voice back.

"And the person who bears this burden is you, Thalia," Sophie added, her eyes looked ready to pop out of their sockets.

I nodded. I did not say more than that. I was afraid that my voice would come out all shaky.

Tremors were zipping through my body, and I was not sure I could stand up straight that moment even if I wanted to.

"I don't think I can take it any longer," I said. I had promised myself I was not going to cry since I walked into this nightmare but it seemed I was not going to be strong enough for even that.

My voice was a little higher than usual, but steadily I realized I was gripping the edge of the table with both hands, and relaxed them.

"What about the stone?" I asked, "what does the stone mean?"

Chapter Fourteen

"I don't get it." Sophie said, as we got our two scoops of ice cream each. We stood opposite the library building in Mr. Olivia's ice-cream shop, which sold only ice-cream cones - obviously. Mike had decided that we come here instead of walking all the way to Aunt Hailey's café just for ice-cream cones.

"I'm not really sure what I get now," Sophie confessed licking her ice- cream in a fast but steady way.

"We always seem to hit a dead end every time we find something that should help us," Mike agreed.

"I don't think I can handle this," Sophie said, "sometimes I wish I was back being three years old again. Not a care in the world. When I still watched my favourite cartoon or was fed my favourite crunchy cookies in my favourite cereal bowl."

I stared at her, mouth agape.

"What?" I'm not really the troll or demon fighting type," Sophie added

"Can't imagine why," I said dryly. I turned my attention away from Sophie and gazed at the looming church. The building was so modern that it might as well have been a fire station or a post office. As a church, the only thing that is cathedral about it was the concrete block tower that stood in front. I closed my eyes most of the way and squinted at it from an oblique angle, put me in mind of a steeple. It sat a few blocks from the mall, which only made trying to get more people to come for services on Sunday hard as people seemed more attracted to fashion that to salvation. There were four cars parked in the lot.

"Thalia, do you know anything about a funeral?" Sophie asked

"No. Why do you ask?" I asked absent-mindedly as I kept focus at the church building.

She pointed towards the back of the church. I squinted a little, noticing a group of people wearing all black and they are unusually tall and strangely looking out of place. Then I noticed that there was no priest, no coffin and no one mourning. It was a funeral.

"That's weird," Mike said, "I read the papers this morning and nothing that talked about a funeral."

"Guys I know I sound weird, but that doesn't look like a funeral," I said.

"Neither do the funeral attendees," Mike added

I moved a little closer, my eyes widened as I saw the people clearly.

"Those aren't people, they are trolls," Mike said.

I led the way through the manicure ground, which looked as sterile as the building. On the other side was a small cemetery, with dozens of neat tombstones as if the designer of the church had planned them too. In addition, among the tombstones were the trolls.

"They look like they could use a buffet party," Sophie said.

She was not kidding. Not that I was going to invite them to one, but they were the most disfigured, underfed looking things I had ever seen.

"Come on," I heard one of the trolls say, still unaware that they had unwanted guests.

"The boss wants it before sunset," one of the trolls said.

"Sorry to burst your bubbles," I said, "nothing is going to your boss before sunset or after."

Now they all spotted me, turning almost in tandem. They were taller than I had imagined.

Mike seemed to notice their common build too.

"Wow! They are like demonic basketball players," he said.

"They don't look like trolls," Sophie put in.

"They are well, the higher rank of the troll family. These ones aren't to be messed with," Mike said

"Thanks for letting us know," I said dryly.

The tall trolls moved towards us.

"We were going to take you by force but since you've done us the service of coming to us, we'll take advantage of your kindness," said one of troll that looked like their leader.

"What? Do I look like your troll pet at home?" I asked trying to sound bold, but I was not. I do not think any other person in my shoes would either.

"Wise words for such a stupid girl," said one of the trolls with a gruffly voice.

"You mean you're going to harm a helpless girl. And I thought you had greater height," I said, If I was not in a tight situation right now I would be congratulating myself at that self-rewarding pun.

My words had the intended effect, or so I thought at first. There was a pause in their advance. They looked so thin I could see myself snapping them to bits without a drop of sweat. They began to walk towards us again.

"I think I made them angry." I whispered to my friends.

The words had barely passed my lips when the trolls attacked. I managed to catch the first one by the wrist when he tried to drive his fawns into my throat, and with a spin, using his own momentum to carry him past me, over my hip, and down on the ground.

I was surprisingly strong, but my strength disappeared with a puff. So much for cleaning up behind themselves.

I could barely see Mike or Sophie. Well, Mike was far from powerless, I thought, remembering how he fought the trolls in Mr. Harrison's house. Another troll came unexpectedly, tearing through my favourite t-shirt and ripping the surface of my abdomen flesh. I grabbed the arms of the troll and twisted it, trying to tie them into a bow and at the same time slamming him right against another of his friend, who was behind him.

"Yeah, is that what I think it is?" I asked as I looked at another direction.

The trolls looked towards me, just as I planned it. I kicked at the ankle of the one whose arms I held and felt something snap, which was good. The troll collided with the other disfigured troll. The two of them disappeared. I had to step back to dodge a murderous punch from one of the trolls, and doing so put me within the range of another coming towards me from the side. I caught my leg on something and slipped. I turned round, just in time to see the two trolls charge towards me like raging bulls. I used my legs to slam one the trolls in the guts, which was enough to make them go 'puff'.

I got back on my feet.

"Thalia?" It was Sophie, and she sound scared, "a little help here?" She called out.

I glanced over at Sophie. Three trolls were surrounding her, advancing simultaneously. She managed to get rid of one, but there were still two, uncomfortably close.

I ran over to her, picked up the heaviest stick I could find and with it, hitting the trolls as hard as I could. They disappeared one after the other as struck them with the stick.

"Sophie are you okay?" I asked, letting go of the stick.

"Fine," She assured, "If you don't count being disgusted and really needing a shower."

"If it isn't the trio?" said a familiar voice.

We turned around just in time to see the strawberry blonde hair witch of a troll.

She was dressed in all black just like the other trolls.

"Sorry if I crashed your party, but I have what I need, and I've got to go. Cha-cha," with that she disappeared, and so did other trolls.

"Should we chase them?" Sophie asked.

"No. I think we had enough fighting for one day," Mike replied.

"I think I'm going to be sick," Sophie said.

"What did she mean by, I have what I need? "I asked Mike.

"A bunch of trolls don't just appear here every day you know," Mike pointed out.

"Have I ever told anyone how much I hate grave yards?" Sophie said.

"No. When?" I asked mockingly.

"It's late and I have to get home," Mike said, "see you guys tomorrow."

Sophie and I watched wordlessly as Mike walked towards the church building, disappearing through to the corner.

"What's up with him," Sophie asked.

"Search me," I replied a little concerned myself.

Chapter Fifteen

I stared blankly at my untouched lunch, wishing life could just be as plain and normal as the peanut butter and jam sandwich. It really bothered me that Sophie was already in deep trouble because she was trying to protect me. I hated myself for being a coward and not standing up to my responsibilities.

It was a change and I had to accept. Change was good, but this kind was too impossible. The truth is that I was grateful for Sophie's coming back and meeting Mike. How was I going to fight these evil forces all by myself without help?

Nevertheless, the worst was that Mike had been acting strangely these days, and it was really getting me worried.

"Munch now, worry later," I said to myself.

I ate my sandwich quietly, taking a large bite and swallowing each slowly and afraid I might choke. Something was wiggling around in the back of my mind, and I felt as if I was forgetting something. Something very important.

Picking up my half-eaten sandwich, I ran upstairs to my room. I bent down and reached under the bed for the bulky report. It was not there anymore. Spontaneously, I reached out for my jacket, flung it over my shoulder as I made my way out. I needed to get an explanation for this.

I ran all the way, trying not to ask questions when tempers are high and racing with fear. There had to be a rational explanation. My breath was short and eyes huge as I called Sophie. After the second ring, she picked the phone.

"It is Sophie speaking," her little voice calming me a little.

"Hey! It is me, Thalia, just wanted to tell you to meet me at Mike's house," I said.

"What? Is something wrong?" Sophie asked.

"It is okay! Just come over." I tried to sound calm and collected.

"Fine then, but take care," she said.

"You too," I replied with a spontaneous smile.

I put the phone in my pocket as I walked towards Mike's door.

"What are you hiding?" I demanded the moment he opened the door.

He watched me fixedly as he stepped back.

"Come in Thalia," he said.

"What really are you up to? I want to know," I demanded.

"If you would just come inside please," Mike said, his grey eyes glittering slowly and my boldness suddenly turned to dust.

I swirled around facing him as he stood a few steps away. I stared at him, hot and impatient.

"Can you please take a sit?" He said, as he pointed to the grey sofa next to him.

I sat quietly. The chair was as soft as I had remembered the last time I visited.

"I need an explanation," I said.

That was the only word that I could force out of my mouth.

"I don't know what you mean," Mike replied.

"I know you do," I said, becoming annoyed, "why are you avoiding us?"

"I am not avoiding anyone," he said somewhat guilty.

"Where is the report?" I asked

"It's with me, I told you I wanted to make some research," he replied.

"How come I don't remember?" I asked.

"Maybe you have a lot on your mind," he tried to convince me.

"I don't buy that." I replied.

An awkward silence followed.

"This is not going anywhere, is it?" I finally said after a while.

"Yes!" Mike said with a grim.

"Gee, thanks, but seriously, tell me what's going on," I demanded.

"You're not going to give up, are you?" He asked.

"Nope," I replied.

"I want to fight and destroy this demon or whatever you want to call it, before anyone is hurt," he said, with anger I did not know he possessed.

I stared at him completely stunned.

"Can you please say something?" Mike asked.

"Have you lost it?" I said with an outburst.

"I know you were going to act like this," he slummed back on his sit, seeming to give up.

"How else do you expect me to act? I asked.

"Should I say that it's a pretty good idea, go on do it and get us all killed," I said.

"It is not getting anybody killed," Mike replied.

"Really! Then what will?" I asked.

There was silence, as both of us tried to think things through. Yes, I was being hard on him but no one could actually blame me. For the short a time I knew him, I was beginning to become more caring.

The sound of the doorbell broke the tenseness. Mike got up and walked towards the door, and opened it.

"Hi Sophie!" He greeted

"Hi, to you too," Sophie said with a sarcastic smile.

Mike laughed soothingly, and I felt the calmness. His voice was smooth and I have got used to it, if not that he could sometimes be a jerk.

"Thalia!" Sophie called, stretching out to hug me.

"Mike thinks it's a better idea to fight this demon himself," I blurted out.

Sophie drew back from the hug to stare at Mike.

"What? Are you insane?" She asked, her concerns were obvious and it showed on her face.

"Exactly what I said," I added.

"You can't possibly think you could eliminate these demons alone," Sophie pointed out. She had a disbelieving look on her face.

"You guys just don't understand," Mike said in a disappointing tone.

"Then make us understand," I muttered.

"I mean the event at the park," Mike said, staring at me as if it was important I understood him.

"Where those bonny freaks attacked you?" Sophie asked.

"Yes, I didn't really tell you guys exactly what happened," he looked distrust.

"What happened? Did they hurt you? "I asked spontaneously.

"No, but I put your lives in danger that day, I was carrying something I wasn't supposed to carry around," he said and he looked serious. That was beginning to freak me out.

"And…" I encouraged him to continue.

"They took it." He said.

"What exactly did they take?" I asked. I was not going to like where this was heading.

"A dagger," he replied.

"What does a dagger have to do with all this? It's not like he is going to use it to plunge into her heart or something." Sophie asked, completely in shock.

I gave Sophie a shocking are-you-serious kind of look.

"What? It's what they always do in action movies," Sophie tried to defend herself.

"That and more," Mike confirmed, he looked like he was going to be sick.

"So now they have it in their hands?" Sophie asked, trying to get in track.

"Yes!" Mike replied, his voice was shaky as if he was holding back something important.

"Wow! This is worse than I imagined," I exclaimed, as I studied him, lusciously.

"There is good and bad news," Mike said with a sigh as he settled back on the sofa.

"Good news first please," I said, "I could use some,"

"The knife would be useless unless it has the power of the stone, which also derives its power from the full moon," Mike said rapidly, as if he did not really want us to catch what he was trying to explain.

"The bad," Sophie said, this time, we were both losing hope of hearing anything that sounded close to good news.

"It was the stone they had stolen that day in the cemetery," he said, letting that sink in; I could see this was affecting him more than he was letting out.

"And worse still, the full moon will be up today," Mike added, sounding hunted.

"Can this get any worse?" Sophie muttered, she was chewing, a sign that she was nervous.

I sat down, restless again. I was a dead meat; there was no doubt about that. Just as if Mike read my mind.

"It's not the end Thalia," He said.

"There is an advantage we have on our side," he said.

"What?" Sophie asked, I had never seen her snap before, but right now, she is quite close to losing her mind.

"Death," he replied, saying the words as easily as you said puppies or something not as deadly.

"Isn't that on their side?" Sophie said rolling her eyes, as if she was dealing with a dummy and was having difficulty explain why we needed the alphabets in the first place.

"Nope, the death of Thalia would..." he began.

I caught him short, jumping off my chair in surprise and complete horror.

"Me, die? How is that an advantage? They would kill me any way," I said, "Oh God!" Yelling partially.

I did not do well under pressure.

"Thalia, can I finish, please?" Mike said, gently pushing me back to the chair.

I hated that I liked the way he touched me, I really did, but no one should blame me that I was reacting to a young man who could possibly save my life during the worst crisis of my life. I sat still.

"The reason is that if you die you would be useless to them because your soul has to part from the world and go to either of the two places it needs to be," he said, letting us digest this information.

I would never be able to digest anything as easily again, food or otherwise.

"But if you aren't dead, but in everlasting sleep they would be able to trap your soul in the demon's body as long as you live which would be forever." Mike explained.

"So how does that help? It's not like we're actually going to kill Thalia," Sophie commented, she looked quite pale and a bit shaken.

"I thought of that too, but that's not what I meant," Mike replied, giving her a scolding look.

"What exactly do you mean?" I managed to say, Sophie was not the only one who though that any of this was a bad idea.

"We fake your death," he said.

"How is that possible?" I probed.

"He would only be suspicious and I can't stand watching my mum suffer for this," I blurted out.

"We are only going to fake your death to him but no one else, you just have to stay low for a while. About the suspicion, there would be no worry there because your dying is going to happen right in front of him." Mike said.

"And how is that going to happen? It is not like we're going to find him where ever he is hiding," Sophie said, but realized her mistake too late.

Mike nodded with a mischievous smile that I was beginning to hate. It always meant we were going to do something dangerous and stupid.

"No way! That is suicide. We might as well just gift-wrap ourselves," I said with a groan.

"It's the only way this plan is going to work?" Mike tried to reason with me, but there was nothing reasonable about what he was saying now.

"What if it doesn't? And somehow I didn't 'die' or something crazy happens," I said almost yelling at his face in frustration.

"Nothing like that would happen. I have everything planned," he said, smiling. That did not help me one bit, it only fueled the anger more.

"The last time you said that we were almost thrown in jail," I pointed out.

Mike laughed. He really laughed. He was planning my death and he was laughing. Unbelievable.

"Even if it does work, we don't know the place," Sophie said.

I started to get up, and suddenly I found myself gasping for air, as if having a super-fast ball hit you squarely on your stomach. I felt nauseous, a sign that I was about to pass out. My vision blurred and my knees buckled.

I grabbed the chair to balance myself, but I was too weak. I was slowly losing control of myself and went into a momentary trance. Even though I did not know when I slumped, I only found myself standing in a large room with doors at both sides. In the middle of the room, there was a casket, golden.

The place was very familiar, but the temperature was too cold for me to be certain, I mean we are in the middle of a heat wave. I turned, knowing I had not been the one to control my movement this time; I was outside facing the front of the building, looking straight at the sign that read:

"Harry's warehouse,"

"Thalia! Thalia!! Answer me," someone yelled from the background, I could not grab who it was. After sometime, I felt a hard shove.

I opened my eyes. The room had stopped spinning, I was lying on the floor, and Sophie and Mike were beside me with concerned faces.

"Thalia are you alright?" Sophie asked almost reaching out to hug me but Mike stopped her.

Mike handed me a paper cup filled with water.

I drank slowly.

"What happened?" I asked, I still could not see clearly.

"You just slumped," Sophie replied, I could hear the tremour in her voice.

Just as if it was real life, I could vividly remembered what had happened when I was unconscious.

"It's the warehouse at the edge of town," I said without even realizing it.

"What?" Mike asked, looking at me a bit closely now like I had lost it.

"Where Leonard is..." I could not get more than that out as I was still in weak from the shock.

Mike seemed to have understood what I was blabbing about, because he had on this weird look.

"Harry's warehouse," he said aloud.

"Yes!" I replied, breathless.

"How did you know that?" Sophie asked.

She did not understand the communication that had passed between Mike and myself. She does not like being in the dark.

"Because I saw it," I muffled, and that was all I could utter before everywhere went completely black.

Chapter Sixteen

By the time we got out of town, it was late and I knew how much worried mum would be. Therefore, Sophie and I decided that we were going to call our mums and make up a story that we were over at a friend's and that we might sleep over.

For Mike, he had no worries because his parents had gone for a short trip that would last for two days so they can spend some time alone by themselves. Thankfully, though, they did not go with the car.

As we set off that evening, we were all quiet throughout the journey, each one in deep thought of different kind and mine was probably, the most twisted.

Mike had told us the plan earlier. It was quite crazy, but it was better than what any one of us had in mind. Sincerely, I was still very worried about the part where we had to trick Leonard. I mean he might be stupid to think he could rejuvenate a nightmare that tormented the neighborhood many centuries again, back to existence again.

However, who would imagine that mere teenagers like us would easily fool an old experienced man like him. I started to think why I did not have any supernatural powers. After all, in movies and novels it was always like that. You carry the curse and you have supernatural powers to change things.

It would have made things a lot easier. I could just walk in, zap him and walk away. Everyone would have a happy conclusion, but I knew it does not work that way.

Our minds were still running riot when Mike stopped the car a few feet away from the warehouse so that we would not alert anyone of our arrival.

I heard Sophie gulped beside me. The only reason she would ever come here was for me. She was the best of all my friends. I mean, how many friends would want to follow you at night to an abandoned warehouse, which held trolls, demons and lunatics.

We got out of the car quietly.

"You girls know the plan. Stick to it and try not to be easy bait," Mike warned us.

"Okay!" We answered simultaneously.

Sophie and I ran towards the building.

"Thalia!" We were already in the shadows when Mike called me back.

I quickly walked to him. "What?" I asked.

"Be careful," he said, "you too, be careful," I replied.

"That mad man should be six feet under," he said.

"Do not fall into any of his traps. He could be dangerous. If you fall, we fall too," Mike said.

"If anything...," I was interrupted abruptly by Mike as he pressed lips on mine, smothering the words.

He pulled back, leaving me gasping for air and in total shock.

"What was that for? "I asked breathless.

"Sorry, I had to. I will explain later. I promise," Mike said.

"Thalia!" Sophie called from the dark.

"Go!" Mike said.

Horrified by his sudden kiss, I moved spontaneously towards Sophie.

"What's wrong?" Sophie asked when I slammed into her.

"Hmm! Nothing," I said reluctantly, and shook my head as if trying to clear it. This was not the time to think about what just happened.

"I'm okay," I said

We walked to the door and was not surprised that it was ajar. We walked silently into the dark room closely beside each other, aware of everything around us. We headed straight for the door in front of us. I opened it, my whole body shaking from the mere thought of dying

The place was cold; it was like steeping into a fridge. It stunned me because that was exactly how I felt in my dream. I flashed back.

"Thalia? Sophie squeaked, "Is it cold or is it just me.

"It's not just you?" I said, feeling a little chilly.

I wonder why I did not bring a sweater.

"Do you think he's here?" Sophie asked.

"I'm very sure." I said.

"Do you think he's going to come out?" Sophie said.

"No, but I prayed he does," I said.

Before I could finish my words, three thin frames jumped at us. Thanks to my reflexes, I kicked the one closest to me before it could jab at my head.

Sophie screamed as she punch one of the troll in the nose. I used my left leg to kick its leg so it could be unbalanced.

"Thanks!" She said.

"You're welcome," I replied.

The more they disappeared the more they came.

"And you would have, thought I wanted to take a karate class myself," Sophie joked even with the tension.

"Yeah! That is the irony," I laughed punching through a bonny broomstick that broke under my hand.

I noticed that the trolls weren't as strong has the ones we fought the last time

"Ouch! I heard Sophie yell at the other side of the room, the darkness did not allow me see clearly.

"Sophie! What happened?" I asked.

"Hello. Nice to meet you again," the blond haired troll said. I did not know the voice, but it was a girl.

"What did you do with Sophie? I asked.

"Nothing she's just sleeping, happy," the troll replied.

"If you touch her I will...," my speech cut short.

"Oh! Please." The girl said interrupting me.

"I...," I started, but I was struck at the back of my head before I could finish.

I fell and fainted.

"Alavine," someone called.

"Yes master!" Alavine answered.

"Would you bring her in here?" Ordered a voice that sent shivers down my spine.

"Yes master," Alavine replied.

I remained unconscious on the floor.

Chapter Seventeen

"Wakie, wakie!" I heard a soft voice calling, and someone shaking me at the same time. I woke up, feeling someone by my side.

"Sophie...!" I called, thinking it was she.

At the far end of the room, I saw a troll using plastic tape to fasten Sophie to the pipe under a vanity sink.

"I hope you like your five-star treatment," the strawberry blonde-haired troll sheepishly muttered.

"Do you know I hate you?" I said coldly without.

"Thanks," she replied.

"Move away from her Alavine," said a depressed voice.

"Yes master, she replied, and then moved away.

I heard Sophie moaned.

"Are you okay?" I asked her.

"Hell no, I feel like I have been hit by a truck loaded with bricks," she groaned.

"You are awake," said a deep voice.

Still feeling dazed, I tried to clear my eyes. Standing next to me was a man dressed in a black robe and hood. Seeing him made me feel nausea

"He is the very man we were looking for," said Strawberry Blonde.

"Nice to meet you face to face," Leonard said.

I remained silent and did not reply.

"I have always wanted to see the person who had all these great powers," he said mockingly.

"Why are you doing this?" I asked. I wish I had such power, I pondered.

"Power, what else?" He replied.

"You are just full of rubbish. You would actually kill a girl because of power," I said.

"I'm not going to kill you. I'll just put you in a trance," Leonard explained.

"I hate you. You really disgust me," I said in anguish, struggling to break the rope in my hands and legs, as if to get hold of him.

"Have it your way," Leonard replied as he moved away.

One of the trolls quickly closed up and fastened the ropes even tighter; putting a lot of pressure on my skin, so much that any wrong move may lead to bruising myself.

"Thalia are you all right?" Sophie whispered.

"Yeah, I am fine, and you? I hope you are not hurt?" I asked.

"Nope! That Strawberry clown hit me though," Sophie tried to explain.

They turned on the light, giving me a better view of the place. To my amazement, there was the same golden casket I saw in my dream. It sent shivers down my spine. Leonard moved to the casket.

"Isn't it beautiful?" Leonard asked.

It is the most startling experience I have ever had. I spat in utmost disgust, chiding myself and wondering why I got into all these in the first place.

"My lord there is a problem," Blondy said.

"What now?" He asked.

"There is a fire outbreak," She cried out.

"How did that happen?" Leonard asked with a sudden disturbed look.

"I don't know master," Blondy replied.

"Let us quickly get on with this before the fire rages and race down the entire building, and quickly get those things of yours," he ordered.

"To put out the fire?" She asked.

"Of course not, it's too late now and if we don't leave this place right away, we would be caught in the ravaging inferno," he replied.

"It's not too late," she said.

"If we don't go now master, we will all be burnt to death in the fire," Leonard groaned, looking very worried.

"Get hold of the casket and let us get out of here now," Blondy replied.

Just as Mike had planned, it is natural that he would think only of himself when he faces danger. Therefore, it was not surprising when Leonard forgot about us and ran out of the room leaving the casket behind.

The smoke was choking us almost to death and Sophie was coughing out of control.

"Where is Mike?" I asked.

I thought I was actually going to die, as I began to slip away.

"Sorry, I'm late?" Mike apologized, appearing besides us.

He immediately started cutting the ropes on our hands.

"This place will soon explode," he said, grabbing me by the hand, jerking me out the way off a beam that had cracked in half and plunging toward us.

Mike looked at Sophie's instructively and ran out of the house pulling her along.

"Keep going," I said, panting heavily.

We all got into the car and Mike pulled the car out of the parking lot with a great swivel and screeching tire as he drove away. Not one of us made any comment until we were a few meters from the building; then simultaneously, we all turned back to see the blaze behind us.

"The police will be there any moment soon, we have to leave here immediately," Mike said.

Our plan worked. I am sure Leonard would not believe that we actually survived inferno. I am glad we lived to see this moment.

Sophie laughed, finally coming out of her trance.

"It is over, for now," Mike said.

"Damn!" I said, as we both started laughing.

"It is over for now," he repeated.

"Till when?" I asked.

Mike did not utter a word until he got into the car. He drove us back home in absolute silence.

I wondered what the police would think of this. I really would not like to be in their shoes.

Chapter Eighteen

The local and national papers were agog with the news of the warehouse fire, which created huge confusion as police investigators tried to figure out what exactly must have happened that caused the fire. While some people blamed it on rebels, others blamed it on smugglers who had done dirty businesses there and were using a fire outbreak as a mean to hide evidence against them.

"If only they knew exactly what happened, that is, the bitter truth," I mumbled to myself.

It has been a week since the incidence happened, and things were gradually getting back to normal. Well, as normal as normal as could be.

"Thalia! Sophie hadn't showed up for a few days now, have you heard from her?" Aunty Hailey asked.

"Sophie had gone on a day's trip with her parents and had just returned yesterday all by herself," I replied.

My daily routine was anything but normal, as I can only go to two places and nowhere else. It is either Aunt Hailey's diner or home. To add pepper to injury, I have to be in the presence of friends and family members the entire time, as if I was under some kind of parole.

For that reason Sophie seemingly finds an excuse to stay over at my house whenever she pleases, as if I did not have a say any more about when she stays over at my place.

The whole idea of being under constant watch is driving me crazy. I could not even go into the bathroom without someone looking over my shoulder.

I was cleaning the counter at the diner when Sophie walked in, smiling and all.

"What's up?" She asked as she sat on a barstool.

"I'm better, what about you?" I replied, I really tried to sound angry but something about Sophie sucks away the negativity from the air.

"Never been better," Sophie said, practically bouncing on her seat.

"I wish I was not working and I had to wrap myself under the duvet and stay on the bed all day," I moaned

On second thought, I realized it would be a rather choky experience. What really are the options available to me other than go to work or silk at home?

"It's the only way you get to take your mind off things and be safe." Sophie pointed out as if she had telepathic powers. She accurately read my thoughts.

"It sucks!" I exclaimed.

"Ha! Ha! Ha!" Sophie laughed.

"I know how you feel; Mike said I should stay low too," she said.

The mention of Mike's name makes me shiver. My mind went back to the night when he kissed me. Apparently, that only exciting thing happened that day.

"You're smiling," Sophie said.

"So?" I asked.

"You had it bad, didn't you?" Sophie asked with a smile.

"I don't know what you are talking about," I lied, because I knew what she meant.

"You like him, don't you?" Sophie growled emphatically, leaving her gasping.

"No I don't," I replied.

"You can't lie to your best friend, Thalia," Sophie said.

I laughed.

"So?" Sophie continued.

"So what?" I replied feeling confused.

"Are you going to tell him?" She asked.

"Tell him what?" I replied.

"Stop acting dumb," Sophie said jokingly.

"Sophie I can't tell him anything that I don't know about," I said, knowing I was not telling the truth.

"Hmm!" Sophie exclaimed.

I groaned and there was a brief silence.

From nowhere, as if he was conjured, Mike walked in. I was shocked when I saw Britney with him.

She looked stylish and leggy, her long blonde hair bouncing around her slender shoulders.

I tried not to stare at them as they locked hands, swinging it as they approached. I shuddered, seething with jealousy.

Sophie was staring too.

"Oh!" She exclaimed.

I could not breathe; I felt all that happened the night before fading away slowly, was it a fluke?

"Sorry." Sophie broke in, noticing the change in my countenance. "He is a jerk. You deserve someone better."

I groaned. I was just being a fool and I hated myself for it. I do not care what Mike did with his love life.

"Thalia." Aunt Hailey called.

"Yes," I answered.

"Table for three, please," she said.

That same table was the same Mike and Britney sat the other day.

"Aunt, I don't think..." I started.

"It's unnecessary," Sophie interrupted.

"I will do it but…," I said.

"Shut up," Sophie interrupted. Took the pad that was on the counter, walked over to Mike and started a long conversation that seemed like it lasted forever.

She laughed, paused for a moment and continued talking and Mike had this weird expression on his face, as one caught off guard.

Still cleaning, I tried not to let him notice that I saw him watching me. I could not stop myself from stealing a glance now and again. Nevertheless, when my eyes caught his, they did not budge. My mouth dry of moist, I was speechless.

Sophie came back.

"This isn't the last time I'm saying that Britney is a total brat sent from the pit-hole of hell," she said.

"I agree," I said involuntarily, my eyes fixed on both Britney and Mike.

"You know what? I'm going to get over him right now," I said. Sophie just kept looking at me with astonishment.

"What, you think I cannot do it?" I asked.

"No, it would just take time to convince yourself its true," she said.

I groaned.

She was right. I was just being a frustrated pig-head.

I did not sleep well that night. I was restless, thinking about the show Mike and Britney had put up earlier that day. It is not good for my health.

I was still engrossed in my thoughts when I fell into a deep sleep and started with my usual nightmare again. I did not have a clear picture of the dream except that I saw a building, then Leonard and the dumb casket. It was a familiar building.

I woke up and jumped off the bed with a start. The church, I breathed heavily.

"Oh my!" I pondered, staring at the full moon right through the window of my room.

I went to the wardrobe and squeezed into black cut offs with tank top and black jacket. The whole house was quite as everyone was asleep.

I climbed out of my window, tumbling bum first and I scratch my arm in the process. It was freezing outside; it must have been around ten or eleven p.m.

I ran in the dark, happy that I had worn all black dress, so I can hide in the shadows without been noticed. Finally, I got to Sophie's house, about twenty minutes later.

I went over to her backyard and to the window. I picked up a little pebbles, aimed them at her window. Thankfully, Sophie is a lighter sleeper and someone coming to open the window rewarded me.

Sophie's head appeared out of the window.

"Thalia, what are you doing here? Is it not too late?" Sophie whispered.

"I know, but I had a dream again," I whispered back.

"How?" She replied.

I pointed towards the moon. She looked at the direction of my finger and gasped.

"I'm coming down now," she said and disappeared back into the house. Minutes later Sophie reappeared from the back of the house, putting on jogging gears.

"I thought that when the moon was up like this you were supposed to be locked in your room," Sophie said.

"I know, but it pulls like a force and I cannot help it. Each time I slept, I have illusions, which never makes any sense nor help matters," I said.

"Okay, have you told Mike?" Sophie asked. I stood silently.

"You haven't told him. Should we go and meet him now?" She said.

"No, I can do this without him," I said stubbornly.

"Don't let your ego kill you one day," Sophie warned.

"It's not so, I'm just going to see what he's up to, that's all," I said.

"Then what? I think it is better we meet Mike first," Sophie replied.

"Sophie, if you want to follow me I will be glad, but if you're going to hag about Mike, I'm fine on my own," I snapped.

"I'm with you but don't get too hard on yourself," Sophie said.

"Thanks. I know you are in a lot of trouble because of me and I am here muttering about myself. How selfish," I said regrettably.

"Truly," Sophie said, assumingly. "Come on, I have two spare bicycles at the other side."

"Thanks again," I replied as I extended my hands to hug her.

We cycled through the dark, certain that no one saw us. Even if anyone sees us, it will look as if we were exercising, and would not think we are going to visit this mad man that have taken over a dorky church with the golden casket.

We got there, parked our cycles at the other side of the church and we both went to the window closest to us to peep through. We could see Leonard. He was alone with the casket. He seemed to be talking to it.

"Wow! I think the man has finally lost it," Sophie said.

We were too busy watching what was happening inside and not what was going on around us.

There was a quick movement, and before we could turn, there she was, right before us.

"Peek-a-boo!" Blonde haired troll said.

Not giving us the chance to come out the shock, she struck us with two quick chops that threw both of us across the floor of the room, knocking off chairs and tables.

"Not again!" I uttered before finally going blank from the hard chop to the back of my head.

Chapter Nineteen

I woke up to find myself awkwardly placed on a table, both hands and legs securely fastened. I tried to clear my head, because I felt as if I have been drinking in the church. It seemed like I was up on the altar and I am being offered as a sacrificial ram in some sort of ritual.

I looked at both my left and right sides and I saw flashes of gold. It then crossed my mind that I was lying on top of the golden coffin. I squeezed my eye in grief, forcing them to close. Few minutes later, I heard a door open some distance away from me.

"Thalia," called a cracking voice.

"Sophie?" I said.

"Thalia, what have they done to you?" I heard her call.

I opened my eyes and looked at the direction of the voice.

Sophie had only her hands tied. They were leading her to the front pew and a few trolls and their leader had already taken their sits and were staring down at me.

"Thalia!" Sophie screamed again.

She sounded hurt, as if they had beaten her up. I wanted to yell back that I was fine but I could not move my tongue. Apparently, I may have been drugged. I fought to clear my head to regain full consciousness. I was so weak that, performing even moving my body appears herculean.

Leonard came toward me, he still had on his robe but the hood was down. I was shocked to see a younger face than I had expected. He had short sand coloured hair, grey cold eyes, laugh lines and an over tanned face. He smiled deeply like a child who just got a new kite.

"Nice to meet you again," Leonard said.

I only shook my head in disgust.

"Sorry about that, we have to inject you with a small dose of a paranoid drug, because last time you proved to be a very bad girl," he added.

"I had you," I muttered, and would have screamed – if I could.

"You actually thought that you could fool me? A cursed one like you cannot just die in a fire outbreak. It would take a lot more than just a burn-fire to eliminate someone with your kind of strength. I am surprised to see you here again though, especially on a full moon for that matter.," Leonard said.

He shook his head pitifully, and all I wanted to do was spit at him.

"Your little guardian is not here to save you this time," he said as he turned to Blondy and the other trolls.

"Search the area and make sure that fool is not up with his usual pranks again," Leonard ordered.

"Mike isn't coming, he's too smart." I tried to yell, but still felt very weak and terrified.

Leonard dipped his hands into his pocket and brought out a short dagger that looked quite aged.

Leonard followed my gaze and noticed my attention was on the dagger.

"It's an ancient Egyptian dagger, dating back centuries," Leonard said. "It was said to have been blessed by the gods as a gift to the lords of the land, and its pointed edge can pierce through even the hardest bone and it's blades can slice through flesh easily, like hot knife on butter," emphasizing the last part with so much excitement.

"You make me sick," I groaned.

Leonard snapped his fingers and a troll came forward and handed over to him a small sack.

"This is the famous Bloodstone," he said.

He dipped his hand inside the sack and brought out an object. It was the most beautiful gemstone I have ever seen. Green quarts flecked with red jasper. It looked like an ordinary ornament, but in some sense, I knew it held great powers. Leonard fixed the stone into a hole on the knife like a jigsaw puzzle. The stone glittered brightly.

"I feel the power vibrate through me," Leonard said, grinning from both sides of his mouth as he glanced at the dagger.

He walked up the altar stair majestically, slowly and carefully taking every step. He stood right at my front, and started tracing me with the dagger from my toes upward and stopping right at my heart.

"I would like to see your friend there," he pointed at Sophie, "die right in front of you and you unable to do anything."

"But I have decided to keep her as a late dinner snack for our little friend you're about to bring back to life," he laughed mockingly.

I groaned, looking straight at Sophie, what have I gotten her into, I imagined, tormenting myself.

Leonard's dagger caught my attention as he pointed the tip at my heart and applied a little pressure, leaving me in panic and almost breathless.

"It's okay, you wouldn't feel a thing. You're paranoid," he said.

"Master," Blondy appeared from the first pew.

"What again?" Leonard asked, angrily.

"Are you with it?" She asked.

"No," he replied, groaning and pacing.

"Show me what all this is about and you keep an eye on them," he said, looking at the other two trolls.

Leonard and Blondy both walked out leaving only the other two trolls with us.

This would have been a good opportunity to plan our escape, I imagined.

A few minutes later, a hand came over my mouth and silenced me as I attempted to yell.

"Don't move," whispered a familiar voice. I just shook my head defiantly.

"If you're trying to be difficult, this is not the time," Mike said.

I turned and his face was right next to mine. My eyes bulged frightfully.

"How did he know?" I thought panickingly.

He saw my expression and tried to explain.

"I told you once that we are connected, it's like GPS," he said jokingly.

I turned to Sophie and again to Mike. He get the message. Sophie was lying on the bare floor, looking lifeless.

"It's okay, she is just acting," he said, getting out something from his pocket.

"You are the one that needs to be help," he said, hidden well behind the coffin from the trolls view.

"Here, drink this," he said placing the tiny bottle to my mouth and pouring its content in three little drops.

"It's okay! It will revive you," he said, keeping the bottle back in his pocket.

He untied the ropes that fastened my hands and feet.

"The antidote will take time for you to fully heal. So just stay put," Mike said.

Sophie, coming out of her slumber, and with vengeance, gave one of the trolls a hard sidekick that threw him flat on the floor with a loud bang, taking the other by surprise.

"Stay here," he said, running toward Sophie to assist her, as two other trolls ran inside to check Sophie where she was on the floor.

The antidote was working. I could feel my nerves move, my breath uneven and my heart stopped racing. For a test, I tried moving my fingers and was quite surprised it moved.

I watched Sophie and Mike to take on the two trolls they seem to know what they were doing, Mike especially. It was as if he had been fighting trolls all his life. I wanted to join them, but my legs where still frail.

"So we have another uninvited guest," Leonard's voice boomed from the church entrance, obviously angered.

Chapter Twenty

"It's like we are going to be having a party," Leonard mocked.

"Well, I'm very sorry I forget my party years," Mike muttered distastefully.

"Bad. It seems like the cursed has been saved," Leonard said walking toward me.

Though I had gained back my strength, I pretended, wanting to catch Leonard by surprise, though Mike and Sophie could actually do better.

"Do you mind if I bring more friends?" Mike said as he smiled.

"Why should I?" I replied.

"I have only one answer, you have been punked," he said.

Immediately Mike finished, some people wearing red robes with hoods on, appearing from all the entrances.

"You brought the whole party along. Hmm...! Interesting." I replied.

"Too bad you are out-numbered," Leonard said with a trace of fear in his voice.

More Trolls appeared all around. We were truly out numbered.

With Leonard's mind on the battle in front of him, I decided to take my chances. With calculated quick movements, I jumped off the casket, ran head long with Leonard, and managed to grab the dagger before he caught up with me and threw me hard against the wall that I felt I had cracked a few rib bones. I got up swiftly with my eyes locked on to his.

At least I had the dagger.

"Alavine!" Leonard screamed.

"That's a really bad name to be called, don't you think?" I said, tauntingly.

Alavine appeared before me, with a weird smile.

"I love my name, it's just fine," he said.

"Let's see about that," I said, as I released a hard hammer sidekick to Alanine's head, the other barely launched as pain shot through my leg.

She was worse than those bony trolls all put together. It was like kicking a brick wall.

Alanine's lips stretched into a wild grin, I dropped back, and ready for whatever Blondy had to give. She released a kick to my shoulder that knocked me down.

I rocked back on my shoulder and leaped to my feet in a smooth and switch movement. Mike on his side, was battling the big fellow while Sophie was giving the trolls in red robes a good fight and they were all doing a great job of it.

"Is that the best you can do?" Alavine said, laughing, and you could feel the evil in his laughter.

I eyed her grimly.

"Small things come in big packages, have they ever told you that?" I replied.

"What, you think you can beat me?" She sneered.

"Just calling it how I see it." I replied.

Alavine rushed towards me, throwing rapid and powerful punches with both hands. I blocked furiously and I tried a leg sweep, hoping to gain a little ground.

She jumped slightly above it and lunched a roundhouse kick to my chest. I was sure of losing some of my rib bones.

I sailed back toward the wall and with a desperate twist; I managed to flip backward in midair, striking with my feet instead of my head. It dropped Blondy painfully to the floor, leaving her breathless as I slipped by her right side while the other troll turned away to avoid being hit.

I slammed one hand into the floor, stopping her slide, and delivered a hammer kick with my right leg. Still holding the dagger, I aimed it right at her torso and her eyes went wide with sudden realization. Too late, the dagger made a nasty deep cut right through her body and she collapsed.

"Yap, this is the best I have got," I said.

"No!" Leonard exclaimed.

I looked at Leonard in shocked and I started walking towards him. "It is the end Leonard, give up now," I said, still holding the dagger.

"It is not the end." He groaned.

"Please, Leonard I don't want to do this. I really do not," I said.

"No you don't," He replied.

He charged right at me. With great reflex, I threw the dagger at him and it cut right through his heart.

He made a loud agonizing and shrilling sound, and instantly turning pale.

What would have happened to me a few minutes ago had just happened to him. He slumbered next to my feet and he was still breathing, but clearly, these were his very last breath.

Have an everlasting sleep, rest in peace Leonard, I thought.

The bloodstone glowed as it drained Leonard's body and his soul off his body. I knelt by his body, fatigued and devastated.

"Thalia!" Sophie called.

I looked round and Sophie was standing just a short distance away from me, staring at Leonard body in horror.

"Are you okay?" She asked as she came to give me a big hug.

"I am fine, but I feel like hurling," I managed to say.

"I know how you feel," She said looking pointedly at Alavine and Leonard.

Sophie released me. The red robes had fought and won. Mike had Gason, the biggest amongst the troll, crumbled lifeless on the floor.

Mike came over to us with five other red robes behind him and he knelt down beside me.

"You did pretty well," He said, smiling.

"Yeah." I said, as I turned to him and started frowning stupidly.

"Yep, you could say that again. But I am not going to scold you yet," Mike said.

I laughed. It felt nice to let the chill pass.

"There are some people here to see you," Mike said, pointing to the group behind him.

"Good to meet you, Thalia, it's an honor?" Said one of the red robes. He pinned down his hood revealing his face. He must have been sixty.

"Thanks!" I said politely.

"I like you to meet my right hand subjects," he said.

They all brought down their robes and I noticed a man and woman first, they looked familiar.

"Hey! Mum, dad!" Mike exclaimed behind me. My eyes broadened.

"You are Mike's parents?" I asked.

"Yes, and it's truly an honor to meet you." They both replied.

I looked at them for a while and noticed the other face. Mr. Harrison? He stood there, still looking very healthy.

"Mr. Harrison? I cried out, shocked to see him here.

"I am still holding you for that silly prank you played," he joked.

I laughed, and stopped when I saw someone else. I stood still; it was Ryan this time, standing there in front of me, wearing a red robe just like the others. I could not believe it.

"Ryan, sir." I said to the older man with a slight nod.

Mike and the others including Sophie walked away leaving only the two of us.

Things felt very awkward.

"It...." He stammered.

"Hi!" I greeted.

"Hi! I knew this would be awkward, I am sure," he said, defiantly.

"I'll manage." I replied.

"You want to talk?" He asked.

"Sure," I said.

This scene confirms my impression of him from the beginning.

"I am a peace maker," he began and when I did not answer, he continued. "It is a...."

"I know what you mean, Mike has explained." I interrupted.

"Yeah, hmm! I wanted to tell you this a long time ago, but couldn't bring myself to tell you till now," he said.

I rolled my eyes.

"It was an assignment at first," he said, "in marrying your mother."

I stared at him, shocked. I really did not expect my accusation to be true. I wanted to yelp.

"Wait!" He stopped me when I opened my mouth to speak.

"Yes, it was all fake at first," he added.

I stared at him, a little confused.

"But I fell in love with your mum. It was hard for me not to. Your mum is lovely, beautiful, caring and understanding, and I fell into her trap and could do nothing but stay," he said, "I know I may not have been the best father for you, but I promise to make it up to you."

I wanted to reject his offer just as I did countless number of times in the past, but I could not do so. I realized one thing though, that sometime our feelings does not always represent the truth.

I looked at Ryan as he waited for me to decide. I think he deserves to be giving a chance. Everyone deserves one, I sighed. This was harder than I thought.

"Please take me home," I said, "dad."

He smiled, bustling with joy.

"What?" I asked, in an attempt to make him frown.

"Nothing," he said, still griming.

"We must find a way to tell mum the truth," I said.

I could not possibly live without mum knowing who her daughter really is.

"It's fine with me," Ryan replied.

"It has been a long and hectic day," I said.

He nodded.

"Let's go home," he replied.

Epilogue

Everything was back to normal again, this time for real. The church fire incident that occurred was said to have been carried out by robbers. It was reported by the media that, the place was attacked without stealing a single item. It was as if the peacemakers covered up their tracks very well, everything except the fact that I still had my new life.

Now that I was out of danger, it felt good to have brought out the real me, and Sophie had gone on a few days trip with her parents to spend the last of the summer holiday as school approached. Mum was shocked off her spine when she heard about how Ryan and I had reconciled though, we had not told her the true reasons.

The casket and its master, Leonard, kept safely away from any physical contact at a place where no one could find them.

Mr. Harrison is in the retirement home now, living what is left of his old age. The best part is for the last; at least, that is what they say.

Mike and I are together now. It felt right and wonderful. Mike had explained that the reason why he left with Britney was that he had been so confused the last time we kissed. The rumour that I never wanted him was false. It feels like a fairy tale when you get what you want and more so at the very end.

All these thoughts rush through my mind as I mopped the floor of the diner, and just as if I had conjured him, Mike walked right into the diner wearing blue jeans shirt and jacket.

"Hi!" He greeted, walked up to me.

"Hi!" I replied, hugging and kissing each other and loving the feel of him like butter mint and strawberry.

"Busy?" He asked, as we pulled back.

"I was until you walked in," I joked.

"Do you mind dropping that mop and coming for a walk with me?" Mike asked.

"Definitely," I said, dropping the mop.

"Let me go and get my jacket and inform Aunt Hailey, that I will be closing early," I said.

"Please do that." Mike said, kissing me again before I walked to the back door.

As I was picking up my jacket, a beautiful thought crossed my mind. Who says mishaps do not end with a happy ever after?

It all started with a single stone, the bloodstone.

The End

NOTE FROM STEPHANIE OYINKI

What inspired me To Write Bloodstone!

Bloodstone for me is a captivating dialogue that attempts to capture the adolescence lifestyle and their mindset, representing their thoughts, behaviours and reasoning, often wrapped in exuberance, sometimes-exhibiting comic tendencies and wishful fantasies that represents the life and style of teenagers.

Sharing this dialogue brings to mind and reveals the peculiarity of the adolescence child and their fears, risk and threats they often have to put up with, for many it remains buried in their thoughts, and for some they find expression in many different ways.

I find expression in writing about my dream, a fantasy world created by me, which I wish to express and share as a way of embracing and encouraging the millions of teenagers around the world. Letting them know that they are not alone and that they should be free and courageous, enough to tell their own story of an interesting world that reside inside of them.

As you read the book Bloodstone, every new chapter you turn to reveals something familiar. A reminder you of a relationship, a peculiar thought action, emotion, romance, fears, sentiment and even hatred.

Do enjoy your reading as you look forward to my next book, which I assure you will be equality exciting and entertaining.

Quotes

QUOTATIONS FROM QUOTE-ME

"It is hard for successful people to find help. It is believed that they can always take care of themselves,"

"Success takes you to the top where sycophancy is pre-dominant,"

"Love is a spirit that overwhelms you like a charm".

"Talk is cheap when addressing idiots, but expensive for informed audience,"

"When the race is hot and you desire to eliminate all contenders, remember that you need them to run another race,"

"It is only a foolish fisherman that lets off a big catch because of the plash of water,"

"Those who add little or no value to your life are often those who expects much from you,"

"You can't fully appreciate your capabilities until you put yourself to the test,"

"Success is the reward for endurance and persistence at what you do,"

"Evil coated in gold and glitters will always over-shadow good covered in sack and ashes,"

"Life will always provide for those who sow a seed and wait patiently," "Forgiveness is the antidote for healing broken hearts,"

"The things that matters most are often those we take for granted,"

"Opportunities are useful only to those who are available and pre- pared,"

"War is a game of death that is better not to start because it never ends without loss of lives,"

"The past is history you can't change, but the future is a story you can rewrite,"

"Difficulties remain a life-long challenge for those who worry, but those who seek solutions improve their situation,"

"We all are connected in an intricate web of life. Your lack of support to others only reduces your own chances of growth,"

"Love is a gift of the heart from one to another,"

"Success is measured by your ability to keep failure under control,"

"To be quick to promise and slow to fulfill is a sure way to build bad reputation,"

"A promised broken by one person, dashed the hope of another," "Criticism is a cheap skill that even idiots possess,"

Life comes in tides and seasons. Understanding and patience is key to harnessing your full potentials,"

"Life is fun for those who are free-spirited. Letting the past go helps create room for the future,"

"Evil is like a shadow, always casting your dark side behind you,"

"Secrets are either too precious to share or too shameful to divulge, either way, they are never kept forever,"

"Your present position, either up or down, is determined by your will or lack of it,"

"Every person has two lives, a public and a private life; rarely are both the same,"

Printed in the United States
by Baker & Taylor Publisher Services